W9-CKH-541

HACKS AT LUNCH

HACKS AT LUNCH

A Novel of the Literary Life

Mary Bringle

St. Martin's Press
New York

 For information, address St. Martin's Press, 175 Fifth Avenue, New York, N.Y. 10010.

Design by Doris Borowsky

Library of Congress Cataloging in Publication Data

Bringle, Mary.
Hacks at lunch.

I. Title.
PS3552.R485H3 1985 813'.54 85-10064
ISBN 0-312-35637-4

First Edition

10 9 8 7 6 5 4 3 2 1

To every writer who has ever used a pseudonym.

Here lies poor Ned Purdom, from misery freed,
Who long was a booksellers' hack;
He led such a damnable life in this world,
I don't think he'll wish to come back.

—Oliver Goldsmith

HACKS AT LUNCH

1

Not Eugene O'Neill's

The place where the hacks assembled for lunch on alternate Tuesdays was called Eugene's. It was an undistinguished bar that served indifferent food at lunchtime, and usually abandoned all pretenses of being a restaurant when the last lunch customers returned to work. No one in living memory had ever ordered food during the evening hours; then Eugene's became what it had always been destined to be—a working-class watering place surrounded by shops and cafés of an increasingly genteel stamp.

The owner had given much consideration to the naming of his establishment. His last name was McCloy, but he felt that a bar called McCloy's would, in Manhattan, swiftly sink to obscurity. Much better to employ his first name. He cherished a conviction that the hacks had chosen Eugene's for their meeting place as a way of paying homage to Eugene O'Neill, but the truth was more pedestrian. The founder of the Tuesday lunches, a man called Frier, had once lived a block away and found Eugene's most convenient for these bi-weekly trysts. Frier had long since defected to the West Coast, but the current group remained loyal and came by bus and subway from all quarters of the city—in one case all the way from Brooklyn—with a touching determination.

It was a tradition that perfectly suited all concerned. Although the hacks were never in evidence after dark, when Eugene's real clientele began to assemble, their presence was always felt, at least by him. McCloy frequently had one of their new paperback originals stashed behind the bar, suitably inscribed. "To Gene with affection and gratitude—Douglas." Or, "This could be the big one, Mr. McCloy—keep your fingers crossed! Love, Clare."

At first he had displayed them impartially, these books with their brave, gaudy covers featuring flaming bombers, wagon trains, women fleeing sinister mansions, or large-breasted hussies in ripped gowns, refusing to honor one book above another. He was proud of his writers because they were good enough to have their words committed to print and bound between covers—although not, alas, hard covers. If one of his customers should mildly remark that a book looked trashy, he always had the perfect rejoinder. "A person has to eat," McCloy would say. In the last few years he had stopped showing the books, sensing that his customers would always misunderstand, but they remained in his custody, tenderly kept. His secret library.

For their part, the hacks liked Eugene's for a variety of reasons. It was cheap, for one thing. The long bar in front was handsome but scarred, and nobody fashionable ever sat there toying with Perrier and lime beneath the steeplechase prints and framed maps of Ireland. Nobody had ever been heard to order a wine spritzer. Best of all—six-figure advances on novels, book-club sales, movie rights, and publication parties were topics never discussed in carrying voices from the bar. During the hours the hacks lunched—from two to four in the afternoon—the place was nearly empty.

The hacks sat in the back room, which was not so much a room as a rectangular space in the rear, paved in white and black tiles. They occupied the largest of the four tables, over which hung a fake Tiffany lamp. Their Bloody Marys reposed on Harp lager coasters and their cigarettes were accommodated by plastic ashtrays. The menu was chalked on a blackboard that had belonged to somebody's child in grammar school. The menu never varied, except for the soup du jour. A diner at Eugene's could choose an omelet, a burger with or without cheese, a bowl of chili (canned), a mixed green salad, a salad of spinach, bacon, and mushroom McCloy had added to the menu after strolling up Columbus Avenue and studying the trendier cafés. The first day it had appeared on the blackboard he had taken a ribbing from one of the hacks: "What next? Can quiche be far behind?"

The writers were uneasy about any hint of change at their meeting place because, like themselves, it was neither one thing nor another. The fact that the draft Guinness was cold, bowing to Americanized tastes, reminded them of their own predicament. Just as Eugene knew the Guinness should be warm but kept it cold to suit his customers, so they altered their ideas and tempered their words to suit their reading public. This spirit of compromise, so evident in the running of Eugene's, was less evident in the attitude of the hacks. They could be spirited and quarrelsome, or morose and self-deprecating. What they could never be, by an unspoken rule, was laboring under the delusion that in a better world they might have been gathered in Stockholm to receive the Nobel Prize. Hadn't they called themselves hacks before anyone else could?

Grievances were aired with wit. The victim of an injustice was careful to preserve the humor of the situation; no matter how much sympathy the others showed, the hack with a grievance struggled—sometimes with difficulty, but always successfully—to seem amused, impassive.

Clare Connolly, who had a range of pen names so vast McCloy was dazzled, once explained the nature of their business to him.

"We are soldiers of fortune, Eugene. Mercenaries. We do our best for whoever owns us at the moment."

"Knights."

"Knights," said Clare, pleased, "but not Crusaders."

It was Clare who arrived first on a cheerless Tuesday just before St. Patrick's Day. Spiritless snowflakes whirled in spiral drafts against a dun-colored sky, melting before they could alight and creating a false impression. Winter was dead and spring had been put on hold. It was no-weather, thought McCloy, and from the color of the sky it could be any time at all between dawn and dusk.

McCloy saw Clare picking her way up Broadway, deceptively large in her down coat, her booted feet fastidious as she dodged cindered lumps of mysteriously unmelted ice and objects of a more sinister nature. A bright orange wrapper—McCloy thought it was from a Reese's Peanut Butter Cup—whirled up and struck her in the torso. Clare batted it away with an expression of alarm and continued on her way. In the protective coat she looked like a walking teepee. McCloy knew her dainty progress toward his establishment was caused by her extreme myopia. Clare could not see well and seldom wore her glasses. This uncharacteristic, small vanity produced in her a vulnerable air that was false but appealing.

"Hello, hello!" she cried, entering on a blast of marrow-chilling air. Three old men in cloth caps—the only customers at this hour—hunched their shoulders in protest but registered her arrival in no other way.

"Hello, Clare." McCloy watched her approach the bar. He felt he ought to leap out from his post, take her by the elbow, and steer her to safety.

"Am I the first?"

"You are." He always found it marvelous that the writers lunched so late; there was a kind of glamour to it. They could make their own hours. Freedom was one of the perks of their trade.

Clare's eyes had adjusted to the gloom. They widened as she took in the cardboard shamrocks hung over the bar. On the week of St. Patrick's Day the shamrocks made their appearance, together with a festoon of green crepe paper that culminated in a hand-lettered sign hanging over the cash register. The sign read *Slainte!*

"When is it, Gene?"

"Day after tomorrow."

"I always forget. Inevitably. I'm forever setting out to go somewhere on St. Patrick's Day, utterly oblivious, and getting caught in huge traffic snarls. Buffeted by rowdy high school kids from New Jersey. Slipping in pools of vomit."

"It must be a trial." Much as he liked Clare, he put a hint of reproach in his voice. She, alone of all the hacks, was nominally Irish. She seemed to hear the slight change in his voice, or perhaps she detected the stiffening of the old men's shoulders, because she was instantly repentant. Instead of going straight to the back room, she took a stool at the bar.

"Well then, Mr. McCloy," she said, sliding into the colloquial, slightly affected tone she sometimes used, "How's about you and me lifting one together before the others arrive? This one's on me. I'll have a shot of Paddy's."

McCloy smiled and spread his hands to show that the drink was on the house. "It'll be my pleasure," he said. He poured a shot of Paddy's, oily and deluxe, into a shot glass and set it before her. For himself he drew a Guinness. He was a moderate drinker, and many hours remained before he would go home.

"*Slainte,*" said Clare, lifting her glass and acknowledging their mutual Irishness.

"*Slainte,*" said Eugene. Just as the Guinness touched his lips he had a vivid image of what the place would be like on St. Patrick's night, and in the image he planted Clare. She stood squeezed uncomfortably at the end of the bar, perspiring in her down coat, her myopic eyes wide with misery and amazement. The crowding bodies, the noise and smoke were unendurable to her. Who was this who turned abruptly and spilled his drink down her front? Off-duty cops trod on her toes, innebriated lechers brought beery lips close to her ear; she couldn't escape to the ladies room, even, because McCloy's problem sister, Nora, had passed out behind the locked doors. She was growing more wretched by the minute. . . .

He swallowed the Guinness and the image vanished.

"Here comes Joseph," he said, turning toward the window in his confusion. "He's wearing his earphones."

2

The Fate of Frier

"Just try them," Joseph said. "Go ahead, Gene. I guarantee you, you'll fall in love." He was thrusting the little headset at McCloy.

"Man with new toy," said Clare.

She and Joseph were still sitting at the bar, waiting for the others. Eugene set Joseph's Budweiser before him and retreated a bit, leaning back on one elbow away from the proffered earphones. Joseph's face—the sort of face that would still be boyish in ten years, when its owner would be well into his forties—seemed actually to be pleading. The dark eyes shone with zeal; Joseph's furry, chestnut-colored beard almost trembled with emotion.

McCloy had brought it on himself by mildly stating his opinion on the subject of the ubiquitous Sony Walkman. "It's dangerous to go about the city with your hearing blocked," he'd said. "You can't hear the warning signals."

"Go on, Gene. What do you have to lose?"

McCloy sighed. If a grown man, one of his most cherished customers, found it a matter of such importance to share the wonders of his Sony Walkman, who was he to be churlish? He bent his head and allowed Joseph to slip the headset over his ears. Then he straightened up and prepared for the onslaught of sound, but there was a problem. His head was much longer than Joseph's and the light pads slid up to his temples, where they clung like electrodes. Joseph made the necessary adjustments and then, with a flick of his finger, plunged McCloy into an ordeal by music. It was classical music, quite stirring and martial, and it seemed to enter into his very nasal passages in its desire to become all-consuming.

"Not so much volume," he said and then, by Clare's and Joseph's laughing faces, realized he had shouted. The volume was lowered. McCloy bobbed his head in time to the music to show his appreciation. He felt supremely foolish. "Very nice," he said. "Very nice indeed, Joseph. Quite an experience." He could not hear his own voice. Clare and Joseph were talking together now. Joseph was removing his jacket with eager, jerky movements. He was wearing a costly-looking sweater with his usual faded jeans. Earlier, as he entered, McCloy had spotted flashy cowboy boots on Joseph's feet. It occurred to him to wonder if Joseph had come into a windfall. Two weeks ago the Walkman, now the boots.

McCloy knew it was too early in the year for the hacks to have received royalty checks. March was generally one of the leanest months for them. Perhaps Joseph had at last negotiated a hardcover book contract or received part of an advance owed to him for half a year. He would have to wait and see. If Joseph had good news, he would surely share it with them today. Perhaps he was only waiting for the others to arrive.

McCloy glanced at the cloth-capped men guiltily. What if one of them was ready for a refill and had called to him to no avail? But the old men sat, immobile as before, nursing their tankards. Clare and Joseph had forgotten about him for the time being. Little by little the music was winning him over. It no longer seemed an assault. He thought it was Beethoven but he wasn't sure. The string section was going at it now, loud and sweet. So sweet. He turned and let his eyes rove Broadway, imagining that the pedestrians moved in time to the music. The music was investing them with glamour; a woman alit from a 104 bus to a fanfare of woodwinds. Another bus was chuffing in behind the first. McCloy waited to see if the debarking passengers would perform well. He was smiling in anticipation when he felt a tugging at his sleeve. Clare. He dragged the headset off, heard the click as Joseph banished the music.

"The gentleman would like a refill," said Clare, nodding her head in the direction of one of his customers.

Flushing, he went to the man in question. "Sorry, Jim," he muttered.

"I've got all the time in the world," said his customer. "I've got nothing but time." The words were spoken kindly enough, but as McCloy set the full glass down he saw malicious amusement flicker in the old tortoise eyes. It disappeared, like his earlier fantasy involving Clare Connolly, but it had been there.

"Would that have been Beethoven?" he asked, returning to the writers.

Joseph looked up, as if bewildered. He had put the little machine away in the pocket of his sheepskin jacket and appeared to have forgotten its existence. "Oh," he said. "No, Gene. It was Schubert."

"I'm starving," said Clare. "If they don't come soon, I'm going to order without them."

She spoke as if a great horde of compatriots were expected, but in fact the group was sadly shrunken. McCloy could remember when it took two tables to accommodate the hacks. In the glory days, before Frier's defection, they sometimes numbered as many as ten.

"What do you hear from Frier these days?"

Clare and Joseph exchanged glances, as if calculating how much to say about their old leader. McCloy understood that they both envied and pitied Frier for having gone to the West Coast. At the beginning, he had written long, witty letters to the group describing his unhappy life in the cultural desert. These letters always contained venomous, hilarious descriptions of clashes between the urbane, Yale-educated Frier and the high-tech half-wits with whom he was obliged to "take" meetings. Frier would list the things he missed most about New York. He penned laments for mass transportation, restaurants on Mott Street, chatty, rude cabdrivers. He wrote plaintively of what it was like to be with people who *did not read books,* of the stress he experienced in a society where drugs were obligatory instead of a matter of choice. These letters were addressed to Hacks, care of Mr. Eugene McCloy, and read aloud by Douglas Reville when the group had convened.

Eugene found the letters vastly entertaining. Frier always included a message for him, making him feel that he had managed to penetrate two magical societies at one go—by the grace of Frier he was privy to Hollywood gossip as well as being an honorary member of the undiscovered East Coast elite. It was with some amazement that he heard Douglas falter during the reading of one of the letters—had it been the one about the drugs?—and, laying the paper down on the table, make a pronouncement.

"Not only is he being manipulative," Douglas had said, "the son of a bitch is being condescending."

"I get that impression. Definitely." That had been Clare.

"It isn't as if anything he writes ever gets aired. How can you judge someone who's earning in six digits—"

"Five," said Joseph. "The high fives."

"Medium fives," said Douglas. "How can you justify earning that much money writing stuff that never sees the light?"

"Oh, *justify*." Clare made a dismissive gesture with her hands. "I don't care how much he makes—more power to him. What I can't take is how cleverly he conceals his satisfaction."

"And how about those paeans to New York?" The speaker, as McCloy recalled, had been Beatrice what-was-her-name. She had been a lean, racy-looking redhead who wrote children's books that were seldom published. To pay the rent, Beatrice wrote other things, infrequently alluded to as "strokers" by Douglas. She had defected soon after Frier did, but for different reasons. Beatrice had married a longtime suitor and now dwelt in bucolic New Hampshire. None of her books had ever made its way to McCloy's collection, but he had been fond of her. She had a sharp tongue.

"Do you remember that bit he wrote about the divine rights of bag ladies?" she had demanded. "When he said he preferred to take his lunacy straight? Liked his mad folks to thrust their fists to the sky and curse out loud and alarm people?"

An embarrassed rumble of collective remembrance. All of the hacks had made wry, humorous faces as they recalled Frier's bad prose and disingenuous motives in the bag-lady letter.

It had been Sigrid who took the bull by the horns. She, the youngest member of the group, possessed a sort of moral sternness that intimidated all of them.

"Do I hear a motion to censure Frier?" she asked.

"What for?" Joseph, leaning forward excitedly.

"For condescension, disingenuous manipulation, and bad form," said Douglas.

"We've all been guilty of that." Sigrid folded her hands and swept the table with the ice-blue eyes that had prompted Frier to call her the Daughter of the Prairies. Her spine was straight; her legs, crossed precisely at the knee joint in a way that spoke of moral power so great it could afford to masquerade as feminine delicacy, seemed to await their decision. "We must censure Frier for other reasons," Sigrid said. "He is guilty of taking himself too seriously. Worse—he is trying to conceal it from us. That makes him truly reprehensible. Frier has become a double agent."

McCloy could remember watching with fascination while the hacks displayed a show of hands. The vote turned out to be a tie.

Sigrid, Beatrice, and Douglas were for censuring Frier, while Joseph, Clare, and Marvin what-was-his-name (he was a dishonored psychologist who wrote self-help books and articles for *Cosmopolitan*), dissented. It had been himself, Eugene McCloy, who had been called in to cast the deciding vote.

"You are one of us, in a way," Sigrid said. "What do you say, Gene? These letters from Frier are an insult. He wants to have it both ways. Shall we censure him or not?"

McCloy had felt himself go red and hot to the roots of his hair. In his one experience sitting on jury duty he had felt much the same way, but then the judge had instructed the jury with endless patience on their rights and moral responsibilities. He had known to a hair's breadth what was expected of him, what were the rights of the defendant and what the latitude the law allowed. In that instance, a man's true fate hung in the balance. He would go to jail or go free. Edmund Frier's fate was much less dramatic. McCloy was not even sure what a censuring of Frier would entail, but the thought of breaking the deadlock made his chest go taut. He could feel sweat springing from the follicles of his hair; his ears, in the spot where his reading glasses would normally lodge, burned painfully.

Sigrid's clear eyes held him captive. "Aye or nay?" she asked.

"Censure him," said McCloy. "Aye."

Now, two years later, he learned what it was he had conspired to bring about. In Clare's and Joseph's uncomfortable silence following his question about Frier, he discerned the truth. Frier was not mentioned because, to the hacks, he did not exist. He had been eradicated. Whatever obscure demon had prompted McCloy to speak his name, the effect was the same as if he had inquired of his sister Nora the whereabouts of her husband, Brendan, who had vanished from the earth in 1969.

Presumably Brendan, like Frier, was still alive, but no one wished to call attention to the fact. Clare and Joseph were still contemplating a proper answer to his unseemly question, but they were all saved by the arrival of Sigrid. She had barely had time to walk from the doorway to the bar when the door opened again and Douglas Reville entered.

McCloy smiled, relieved and grateful. They were all here at last, all his hacks.

They were only four now.

3

Hidden Messages

Douglas Reville ordered Scotch on the rocks instead of his usual Bloody Mary. When he had given his order he scanned the faces of the others to see if any of them registered surprise. He drew a blank from Joseph, a smile from Clare, which may or may not have indicated surprise, and the infuriating, all-knowing expression from Sigrid that was her hallmark. McCloy, of course, said nothing.

Something upsetting had happened to Douglas, something he would never mention to the others. He lounged in his seat at the table's nominal head—the spot that commanded a view of the bar and the windows beyond—and wondered if he looked to them as he had looked in his mirror before leaving.

"Gene was asking about Ed Frier," Clare said, lowering her voice. "He asked if we ever heard from him."

Joseph smiled. "We didn't tell him Frier had been in town and didn't call us."

"What did you say?" Sigrid extracted her cigarettes from her bag and placed them, with her lighter, in front of Clare's drink across the table. She was trying to cut down on smoking and had instructed Clare to deny her request for a cigarette two out of three times.

"Nothing," said Clare. "You two came in."

"We met at the corner," said Sigrid.

Douglas was instantly alert. Was this Sigrid's way of assuring them that she had not *been* with him? Sigrid lived on the fringes of Chelsea, not twelve blocks from his Greenwich Village apartment. It would be natural for them to meet on the subway, coming uptown to Eugene's, but it had never happened. It wounded him, her swift assurance of an accidental meeting; it was as if she granted him no place in her life beyond the alternate Tuesday lunches.

"Is something wrong, Douglas?" Clare leaned forward, squinting kindly in his direction.

"Of course not. Why do you ask?"

"You look a little—I don't know—melancholy?"

"How can you tell?" Douglas held two fingers up. "How many?" he asked. Everyone laughed, and the drinks arrived. McCloy himself brought them. His backup barman and lunchtime waiter left promptly at one-thirty each day; the hacks had never seen him.

Douglas sipped at his Scotch and tried to recapture the image his mirror had returned to him. Virile, very nearly distinguished, but saved from an academic look by the careful eccentricity of his clothing. His Harris tweed jacket might seem professorial, but his faded jeans and running shoes proclaimed him a man of freedom and leisure. On his head he had worn a flat tweed cap, very like the ones the men at the bar were sporting. Unlike the men at the bar, Douglas removed his cap indoors.

What about the face? Even in the gray northerly light of his Village apartment, it had seemed rugged, appealing. The slightly seamed texture of the skin, the rueful lines around his dark eyes, were appropriate to a man in his early forties. The Harris tweed jacket picked up the color in his full, fox-colored mustache. When Douglas smiled into the mirror, the mustache tilted upward; if he narrowed his eyes and smiled at the same time, he achieved the mocking look so prized in the heroes of romances. He gave Clare his mocking smile now, softening it by puffing his lips at the last minute in a self-deprecating little kiss. He was beginning to feel better.

"Before I forget," said Sigrid. "Who doesn't have a copy of *Fiona's Folly*? Was it you, Douglas?"

Douglas admitted that it was so. That was another thing, he thought. Sigrid had been short a copy last time and presented the two she had to Clare and Joseph. She hadn't written in the books at the table, which meant she had already inscribed them at home. In the privacy of her own apartment Sigrid had made the decision to let him wait a week. Not that it mattered—he would not be reading *Fiona's Folly* because he did not want his own work to be influenced by Sigrid's—but it was another example of—what? He watched while Sigrid spread the book flat on the table, selected a felt-tipped pen, and wrote on the title page in her small, neat hand.

It was a matter of being so easily wounded these days. He felt people were judging him, thinking sly thoughts about him and perhaps pitying him just a little because he had passed the age of forty and still had to borrow money when his checks were delayed. He had read with wrath and incredulity a piece in the paper which stated that a man to be counted a success should be earning twice the amount of his age. Douglas, at forty-two, was not earning so much as his age. This year he would present his tax man with evidence of his failure. He had brought in, through advances and royalties, the stunning sum of $22,000. According to the newspaper piece, this amount would mark a boy of eleven truly successful.

"Here, Douglas." Sigrid passed over the inscribed copy of *Fiona's Folly* with a wry smile. "Poor Fiona looks awfully bored, doesn't she?"

"That's nothing compared to the way the artist did Laird Bruce's legs," said Joseph. "Where are the 'steely knotted muscles of his powerful thighs, coiled beneath the dark, smooth skin, as menacing as the silver dirk flashing at his side?'"

"They're concealed beneath his kilt, of course," said Clare.

Joseph smiled complacently. He had scored points by hinting that he had actually read *Fiona's Folly*.

"I always think 'dirk' is such an irritating word," said Clare. "Why can't they just call it a dagger?"

Douglas examined the cover of the paperback. It had been put out by a packager for whom they had all worked at one time or another. He saw what Joseph meant about the hero's legs. The artist had somehow foreshortened them so that the Laird almost appeared dwarfish. He stood, hands on his kilted hips, short legs spread, grinning at Fiona, who knelt at his feet in a supplicating posture. Her eyes were shut, lips parted in what the artist had obviously intended to be a mixture of terror and unbidden passion, but the effect, as Sigrid had noted, was one of great boredom. The artist had saved his best shots for Fiona's hair (a rippling mane of improbable crimson), her breasts (aggressive twin globes spilling from a tattered bodice), and the gleaming dirk nosing out from the region of the Laird's groin. There was something familiar about the cover. He thought it might well have been done by the same artist who had ruined *Bride of the Cherokee,* one of his own.

He turned to the inscribed page. Here Sigrid had written: "To Douglas with love. I've read every word you've ever written." It was signed with her pen name, Lucinda D'Arcy, and countersigned "Sigrid."

His pleasure at her inscription was ruined by the implied criticism. "Thanks, love," he said. "I'll be reading *Fiona* as soon as I can."

Sigrid smiled her enigmatic smile and asked Clare for a cigarette.

"No," said Clare.

18

Joseph began to tell them about an article he had read. It explained why writers' checks were always late, he said. Giant corporations were hiring experts on cash-flow management, and the writer, as usual, was the one to suffer. Something to do with holding money, accumulating interest, quarter-yearly tax assessments. For the first time, Douglas felt he disliked Joseph. Joseph's boyish face, his goony, innocent air at the age of thirty-three, his curling, foppish beard, all filled Douglas with annoyance. He felt suddenly sure that Joseph was working on a real novel. He might have signed another contract with the packagers, as he claimed, might even now be turning out ten pages a day on the interminable Desert Warfare Series, but he had something else up his sleeve.

"Have you been paid for *Desert Falcons?*" asked Sigrid solicitously.

"Only the first half. They owe me."

"And you're doing another one for them?"

"I've got seventy pages of *Heroes of the Sands* already done."

Joseph spoke shyly—a bride-to-be commenting on the trousseau. This tender new air of Joseph's could not possibly result from satisfaction at prolonging the life of Major Jon "Hawk" Matthews of the tank corps; it could be accounted for by two things only. Either Joseph's sex life had dramatically improved—he had been moping ever since his wife of five years had left him for a man of more promise—or he was dreaming of springing a real novel on the world. Douglas knew the signs—the period of aberration during which one composed glowing reviews that would appear in the *Times* and crafted one's speech for accepting the National Book Award.

Sex, or delusions. Those were the only things that caused a man to nurture subterranean happiness while imagining that others didn't notice.

"If I have a salad and another drink," said Clare, "will that be more caloric than if I have a cheeseburger and no drink?"

"About the same," said Sigrid. "Or you could have the cheeseburger without the bun and a glass of wine."

Douglas sighed. He might as well be lunching with two secretaries. There was something in the grayness of the day that augured badly. He was trying not to think of the incident that had upset him, but his friends were failing to provide distraction. He was about to order a cheeseburger and french fries when the importance of Clare's and Sigrid's remarks on calories hit him. Had the little caloric lesson been intended for *him*? Surreptitiously, he slid one hand under his Harris tweed and pinched the flesh above his belt. He did not encounter a roll of flab as he had suddenly feared, but neither did his fingers pluck in vain.

"Are you looking for something, Douglas?" Sigrid's voice held no irony. Was it possible he only imagined that suave mockery?

He picked up *Fiona's Folly* and put it in the large inner pocket of his jacket, as if that was what he had been intending to do all along.

4

Cruel, Sardonic Lips

With her glasses on, Clare could observe McCloy as he went about his business behind the bar. The others assumed she put them on at a certain point because she wished to see them more perfectly, to judge whether one of their comments was affectionate or tinged with malice, but this was not the case. She knew Joseph and Douglas and Sigrid so intimately it was not necessary to see them in order to interpret their meanings.

McCloy was a different matter. She had seen more of him, these past five years, than she had of her own father, and yet she could not say she knew him. Once she had asked the others: "What do you suppose Gene's life is like, away from the bar?"

"I've often wondered," Douglas had said. He said it in such a way that Clare knew he had never thought about it at all.

Joseph had begun to weave a life for McCloy—five kids, a wife who had once been pretty but was now faded and worn from child-bearing, a brother who was a priest. . . . He had described Gene's family as if he were outlining a character for one of his books, rapidly, predictably, piling cliché upon cliché with gusto. It had angered Clare, and she was surprised at her anger. Only Sigrid had shared her moral outrage at Joseph's scenario, speaking with distaste.

"It's none of our business."

Now Eugene stood at the far end of the bar, arms folded across his chest, seemingly engaged in conversation with one of the old men. Clare studied the way his smile came and went. He had a long, shapely mouth; when he smiled the corners turned up but the lower lip remained straight. He had a way of bending his head when he was amused, as if offering his thinning, pale hair for inspection. He was a plain man, but there were many aspects of his physical shell that were pleasing. His eyes, unremarkable in shape or size, were an innocent, celestial blue. His hands were square and capable-looking, with finely turned knuckles and the cleanest, rosiest nails Clare had ever seen. She assumed he was about Douglas' age, four years older than herself.

"I know you're all tired of Hawk Matthews," Joseph was saying. "God knows I'm tired of him too, but when you're on to a good thing, why ditch it?"

"How many more desert battles can he fight? I mean, there must be a certain *sameness* to tank warfare." Sigrid, as always, seemed genuinely interested.

"Well, I'm going to send him back to the States for a third of the book. Compassionate leave. His old mother is dying." Joseph's eyes closed briefly, as if in grief for Mrs. Matthews.

"Let me guess," said Douglas. "He'll come back to find his wife in the arms of another man. What's her name? Trudy. Then Hawk will have an excuse to screw an exotic belly-dancer when he goes back to Egypt."

"No," said Joseph in a hurt voice. "That's not what I'd planned." There was an embarrassed silence while everyone recalled that Joseph, not so long ago, had been cuckolded by his own wife. Douglas seized his mustache in a stricken gesture but said nothing. To apologize would only make matters worse.

"The readers *like* Hawk," said Joseph. "You know those questionnaires at the end of the book? In the 'Who is your favorite character in the Desert Warfare Series?' space, nine out of ten readers write in 'Hawk'."

"Well, he *is* the main character," said Sigrid.

"That doesn't necessarily ensure favoritism. I noticed in the submarine series reader response was going for the chief engineer instead of the captain."

Clare saw McCloy pace the length of the bar and go into the kitchen to check on their orders. He moved slowly, but with conviction. Not at all like Hawk Matthews, who, according to Joseph, strode across rooms "with the animal grace of a panther pursuing its quarry." Hawk Matthews was a big man, with broad shoulders, lean hips, and the inevitable steely thighs. He had a mane of blond hair (never mind army haircuts) and sea-green eyes that were always reminding people of a polar ice cap—"cold and impregnable." He was a man's man, but because Joseph vainly hoped to interest women in tank warfare and swell his sales, he shared many of the qualities of a romantic hero.

He did not, however, have the "cruel, sardonic lips" of Sigrid's Laird Bruce or Clare's own most recent creation, Cristobal St. John. Hawk was basically your clean-living American soldier, a good man whose heroic instincts were brought to a pitch of incredible courage by the exigencies of war. Laird Bruce and St. John were not good men, or rather they did not *know* they were good until love of a woman redeemed them. Before the transforming power of love humbled them, they were capable of the most astonishing cruelties; because they had never suffered the pain of unrequited passion, they had no pity.

Sigrid had caused Molly MacGregor, a voluptuous crofter's daughter, to hang herself from an alder tree when Laird Bruce took his powerful thighs and gleaming dirk elsewhere. Clare was pondering a similar fate for Josefina, the fiery gypsy girl who loved

Cristobal St. John "with a passion so tumultuous it spread to every fiber of her being and threatened to destroy her."

"They didn't have those questionnaires when I started out," Douglas was saying. "Occasionally some reader would write to the publisher though, and fire off an opinion. I had written two of the Charlie Slattery series—"

"Under which name?" Joseph looked confused.

"That would have been J. J. Sweeney. Before your time. "Anyway, I had just completed the second one—*Death Plays the Numbers*—when in comes this letter from a woman living in Wyoming. She had read the first in the series and she'd picked out this character, very minor, a barber Slatts went to on a regular basis, and she was convinced it was her husband. Her husband had disappeared ten years before, just walked out one day with no word, and although he wasn't a professional barber, he was very good at cutting hair. He always cut their kids' hair she said, and it looked as good as a professional job. His name was John Arthur Clover, and she had reason to believe that the Jack Clover in my book was indeed her husband. She asked if I would send her his address so she could collect some child support."

"How sad," said Sigrid, while the others laughed.

"I had to go through the manuscript of *Death Plays the Numbers* and change the goddamned barber's name, and then it seemed stupid to have the barber in at all if he wasn't going to be a running character, so I just deleted him. Pissed me off."

"You didn't have to change his name," said Clare. "You should have written to her, Douglas. You could have explained it was just an invented name and set her mind at rest, and then you could have had Jack Clover as a running character."

Douglas sighed. "I know. It just seemed I wouldn't have much fun with Clover, knowing there was this pathetic creature out in Wyoming thinking it was her husband."

Clare smiled at Douglas. Just when she found him most trying, something would happen to remind her that he was rather nice really. Poor Douglas. Did he know that he had developed a slight tic in the last few weeks? It was much more noticeable today—a muscle in his left cheek jumped uncontrollably, causing one eye and one half of his mustache to jump with it.

"Listen," said Joseph, "would it be too much if I had Hawk fall in love with a Frenchwoman who turned out to be Rommel's mistress?"

"Rivals in love and war," said Sigrid. "Not bad."

Clare turned her attention back to McCloy, who was coming from the kitchen with two plates. It always pained her that he had to wait on them himself. It took him several trips, and a flurry of thank-yous rose from the table, profuse and artificial as incense.

"Yes, the salad, Gene, thank you," said Sigrid.

"Thanks, Gene, I would like mustard, thank you," said Joseph.

When McCloy set her plate down, Clare saw the fine, sandy hairs on his forearm. It was not a particularly powerful arm, but it was nicely shaped. She remembered the lathe in shop class, eighth grade it must have been, and how it could transform a square block into a smooth, cylindrical shape. The pure white wood had been silky to the touch.

"Thank you, Gene," she said, and removed her glasses.

She had given Cristobal St. John black hair and blue eyes, a winning combination, especially if, as with Cristobal, the eyes were set in a bronzed face and ringed with thick black lashes. Cristobal's eyes were azure, or cobalt, or the color of cornflowers, but when passion gripped him they blazed "like black diamonds mined in Hell" or "flashed their blue hellfire" at whoever had aroused him. Clare knew exactly what it would be like to trail her fingers over Cristobal's bare chest. The flesh would be smooth as marble, warm and hard. She was not fond of hirsute men and had never been partial to Sigrid's heroes because they sported luxuriant pelts of chest hair. Black curls were always peeping from Laird Bruce's open singlet—women twined their fingers in it, pressed their lips to it, shuddered to feel it against their naked, heaving breasts. Clare wondered if Sigrid preferred hairy men or simply thought her readers did.

The whole matter of hair was very important in their trade. For both men and women the colors had to be vivid—a glowing river of golden, honey-colored tresses, a silken spill of raven black, a fiery mane so bright it threatened to sear the fingers of those who touched it.

Nowhere in Clare's and Sigrid's novels was there so much as a mention of the fine hairs that grew on the forearms of human beings.

Clare picked up her fork, safe once more in the protective world of her myopia, and speared a mushroom from her salad. The glimpse of Eugene's arm had been oddly upsetting, as if he had exposed himself to her.

5

Harnessing Sorrow

It had been exactly six months to the day that Joseph's wife, Vivvy, had left him. There'd been a time when Joseph woke each morning knowing how many weeks—then months—had elapsed since her departure, and he thought it was a sign of his improved state of mind that such an important anniversary had slipped his mind. He had only thought of it when he saw the shamrocks over the bar, counted back from St. Patrick's Day, and discovered that it was the fifteenth. Half a year; also, come to think of it, the Ides of March.

On the fifteenth of September, he had come back to his Brooklyn apartment to a scene of desolation. At first he thought he had been robbed, but then it came to him that the missing objects were things no self-respecting thief would take. Gone from the cramped kitchen was an earth-colored flower vase Vivvy had made during her potting phase; from the living room a framed Magritte print and a small, braided rug she had brought from her parents' house in Netcong. The bedroom was the worst. The closet door stood open to reveal Joseph's clothes hanging sadly by themselves; nothing remained of Vivvy there but a bevy of wire hangers. In the center of their bed he discovered an envelope which, when he picked it up in now trembling hands, seemed strangely heavy. When he finally summoned the courage to open it he discovered the reason—she had left her wedding ring behind.

Joseph remembered the real grief, wave after wave of it, that had immersed him as he read and reread Vivvy's good-bye letter, but he also remembered something else. He had never had a communication, in writing, from his wife. They had never been parted long enough in the five years of their marriage to send each other letters, and aside from the hasty, ungrammatical notes married people leave around the house (Went to movies w/Judy back sixish; Could you get T-paper & butter baby?), his wife's kiss-off letter was the only example of her writing he was ever to see. What Joseph remembered, somewhat uncomfortably, was that he had judged Vivvy's prose, even at the height of his sorrow.

Phrases such as "You have always been a dreamer Joey and I can't live on dreams any more" made him feel ashamed for her, as did "A part of me will always love you, but it's better if I leave now, before all the good memories become poisoned." It almost seemed as if she had browsed through one of his novels before putting pen to paper.

"May I have the salt and pepper?" Douglas' voice broke into his reverie with barely restrained impatience. Something was certainly eating at him today. The muscle in his cheek jumped uncontrollably; his outstretched hand seemed to tremble. Joseph passed him the salt and pepper, noting that Douglas still wore his own wedding ring, the one from his second marriage, long dissolved, on the third finger of his right hand. He wanted to say something kind to Douglas, but any hint of compassion would raise the older man's hackles.

Douglas had been a real gem during those tormented early weeks after Vivvy's vanishing act. Douglas had been through it all twice before (although he maintained *he* had done the leaving the second time) and had a wealth of tricks in his arsenal, which he passed on to Joseph.

"Okay," he would say, his voice deep and reassuring at the other end of the phone, "here's what you do. I want you to think of

Vivian at her worst, looking terrible. Rock bottom. Remember a time when you looked at her and had to look away again."

Joseph had been hard put to it to remember such a time, not because Vivvy had been always lovely, but because he hadn't really minded her less alluring moments. Vivvy at less than her best had been reassuring.

"I'm talking blemishes, oily hair, menstrual pallor." Douglas' voice had been intimate, coaxing. "I don't care how good-looking they are—there's always a low point. I want you to fix on that low point instead of romanticizing her, Joseph. Did you ever catch her secretly picking her nose? Plucking a hair from her chin?"

At last Joseph remembered a time when Vivvy had actually repelled him, although it had nothing to do with the sort of vignette Douglas, almost lovingly it seemed, was trotting out for his approval. They had been arguing about money, as usual, and her face had fallen into an alien, old-ladyish look of disapproval, lips pursed in such a way that a deep line had run from the corners of her lips to her chin. She had looked like a puppet—one of those sour little dolls whose head is carved from an apple and dried to a desiccated hardness. Mrs. Altmann, Vivvy's mother, had one of these apple-dolls on her mantel in Netcong. Joseph had always felt, uncomfortably, that there was more than a passing resemblance between doll and owner, and now he saw that Vivvy's gene pool held the threat of an apple-headed wife in the future. He had wanted physically to pry her lips from their trollish position and restore her young face to its normal, unremarkable prettiness.

When he related this incident to Douglas, the latter seemed unsatisfied. "Well, alright," he'd said reluctantly, "remember her with an apple head, then. Sour. Mean. Closed. Every time you get a picture of her all warm and cuddly and sweet and silky-haired, slap the apple head on. Actually, it's a pretty good image after all."

"You think so?" He'd wanted Douglas' approval. He had to offer

Douglas something in return for the experienced counseling he was receiving from a twice-divorced man. In the first ten days of Vivvy's absence he had called Douglas a dozen times, sometimes quite late at night.

"Look at it this way. A woman has a bad day now and then, raging hormones or whatever, you can't really blame her. It makes you feel sorry for her when you're thinking rationally. But Vivian's image here, the one we've selected, is very telling. It comes from her spiritual penury. It is the outward manifestation of her inward conviction that she deserves a free ride just because she married you. You break your ass and do the best you can and it isn't enough, so she gets some new lover to rent a U-Haul and clears out while you're in the city pitching a new book. You telling me you're gonna spend the rest of your life mourning over a tight-fisted, mean little twat who doesn't even have the guts to confront you openly?"

Vivvy had worked as a secretary in lower Manhattan; far from expecting a free ride, she had been almost demonically industrious. Joseph had flinched at hearing her called a twat, but he supposed it was part of the therapy. Anything that helped still the appalling tidal wave of loss threatening to drown him in those days he welcomed with gratitude.

"Okay, Douglas, I'll work on it. Thank you. I think I'm okay now."

"Anytime, buddy."

Clare was asking him something. He only caught the last few words. Leaning toward her, feeling embarrassed, he asked her to repeat her question.

"I was just wondering if you ever try to write with the Walkman on?" Clare could never ask a question simply. Now, inclining toward him with one hand cupping her sweetly curved cheekbone, her great dark eyes fixed on him as if she were begging for her life or trying to seduce him (it was her blindness, he knew), she elaborated.

"I know you bought it for the subway, those long trips from Brooklyn, but—well, it would be tempting to try it at the type-writer I should think."

Joseph was amazed that the question should come from Clare. In his imagination it was always Sigrid who could see into men's minds, ferret out their motives. He was now faced with a moral dilemma. It was too early to tell the whole truth, which was only now emerging. If he told only half the truth, would that make him disingenuous, like Frier? He opted for half the truth, telling himself that he was a scientist caught at midpoint by his colleagues in the course of a dangerous and revolutionary experiment. For *their* sakes, he would be devious.

"It doesn't work, actually. It fools you."

"How?" Sigrid, alert, gathering information. It would not have surprised him if she had withdrawn her felt-tip from her bag and jotted his comments on her napkin. She held a french fry in her fingers with delicate precision; she bit it neatly in half and chewed, never taking her pale, prairie eyes from his face.

"It seduces you," said Joseph softly. "All that gorgeous music, just for you, in your head alone—it makes you feel exalted. You end up writing lines for Hawk as if he came out of Proust."

"Proust? Really?" Douglas was censuring him.

"You know what I mean." He turned back to Sigrid. "What if Fiona suddenly grows beyond herself? Talks back to the Laird like a Jane Austen heroine? That's what the music does. It encourages you to think you're writing—" He faltered.

"Real stuff," said Sigrid.

"Yes. Real stuff. Real novels."

"I've had that," said Clare, "without benefit of a Walkman."

"Exactly my point. We've all experienced a love for our work that's not—commensurate—to what we're writing. That's not appropriate to the audience. Right? And then we snap back and remember the questionnaires and the market and we tone it down."

"Hold it," said Douglas. "This great, moving stuff you write under the influence of music composed by geniuses—does it hold up in the morning? Is it Proust or is it Velveeta?"

"It's slop," said Joseph. "Better than Velveeta, though. Truly first-class slop. Not appropriate for anything."

"I think I know what you mean," said Clare, returning to her salad. "It's the same as when you try to write when you've had too much to drink."

It was not at all the same, but Joseph suddenly felt his bladder full to bursting. He excused himself and shoved off to the men's room. Standing with his hands braced on the mint-green wall, feeling his perfidy ebb from his body with the poisonous stream of urine, Joseph shored up his secret by calling to mind the tidy stack of typewritten pages in his Brooklyn apartment. They were stored in a special folder, held in another drawer, away from the Hawk material lest they become contaminated. He had already chosen the epigram for the novel that chronicled the dissolution of a modern American marriage. It would read, simply, *For Antonio Vivaldi*.

As he was zipping up his fly, Joseph saw a new graffito that had been scrawled on Eugene's carefully maintained lavatory walls. McCloy's customers were not what you would call a literary crowd, and Joseph had to read it several times to make sure of the wording. Sure enough, someone had taken the time to write, above the urinal, HARNESS SORROW. Joseph laughed softly in delight. It seemed an omen, expressly designed for him.

He fumbled in his pockets for a writing tool, and finding none—just as well, he would feel guilty defacing Eugene's walls—he addressed the graffito aloud.

"Go for it," he said. "Harness it, and then just . . . fucking . . . *go for it!*"

6

Her White, Heaving Bosom

Sigrid watched Douglas bullying his food. He ate angrily, did Douglas. Often he tapped too much catsup on his french fries and then punished them for his excess by tormenting them with the tines of his fork. Today he had ordered Eugene's chef salad for the first time. He had eaten all the little egg halves and strips of ham and turkey straight off, and seemed surprised when nothing remained but lettuce and those pale, depressing tomatoes people in New York tolerated. Now he was digging through the greens with seeming fury, hotly pursuing the treasures forever concealed from him. Screwed again.

A woman Sigrid knew maintained you could watch a man eating and know how he would be in bed. By her standards, Douglas would turn out to be short on foreplay and brutish and bewildered during the actual act. Sigrid did not particularly subscribe to her friend's theory, but she saw how it might apply in another, more important direction. Men who were writers *wrote the way they ate.*

Pleased with the possibilities for amusement inherent in this axiom, Sigrid asked Clare for a cigarette.

"But you haven't finished eating," said Clare peevishly. Nevertheless, since it was the third request, she handed over one of Sigrid's cigarettes. Sigrid lit the cigarette and inhaled with pleasure. Joseph returned from the men's room and slid into his seat, wearing the secretive, happy look he'd brought with him today. Joseph handled his food with respect, as if he felt privileged to be allowed to eat at all. His hand grasped the crescent of cheeseburger bun tenderly; he conveyed it to his mouth as if it were a flute.

What about women? Could you tell? Clare was just now squinting at a french fry, trying to determine if the darkness apparent to her myopic gaze meant that it was too burned to eat. There was an asthetic problem here. Clare could hardly whip her glasses on to pass judgment on a french fry, and the alternatives were even less pleasant. She could bend her head, nearly grinding her nose in the plate, or she could lift it to within an inch of her eyes and appear greedy and foolish. Wisely, she abandoned it and selected another. The theory was beginning to seem perfect. People wrote the way they ate. In Douglas' angry haste, Joseph's respectful timidity, and Clare's deliberate refusal to see the world as it was, Sigrid could detect the flaws and glories of their writing styles.

"How do I eat?" she asked them. "How would you describe the way I eat my lunch?"

"How vain you are," said Douglas. "How should I know? You pick up your food and put it in your mouth and chew and swallow."

"Wait," said Joseph. "That's a really interesting question." He took a sip of his drink and regarded her with dark, searching eyes. Sigrid saw a frisky bubble of foam on his mustache, of which Joseph seemed unaware. "You eat the way you do everything else," he said. "Very deliberately. With grace. You never seem especially hungry, but I've noticed you don't leave anything on the plate, either. Vivvy, for example, always left a bite—usually something she didn't care about, like a slice of cucumber, but sometimes the last bite of something like lasagne, which she was crazy about—because her mother told her it was good manners. I always thought it was terribly affected, myself."

"You *are* deliberate, Sigrid," said Clare. "Also, as Joe said, graceful. My impression has always been that you eat the way a person does who never has to worry about gaining weight. It makes a difference."

"Christ, what has this group come to?" Douglas raised both hands in supplication. "Is this a parlor game?"

"I'm evolving a theory," said Sigrid.

"Add this to your theory," said Douglas, lowering his voice and speaking in tones of humorous venom. "You may chew and swallow, sweetheart, but you don't shit. Is that what you wanted to hear? You don't shit."

"My, Douglas, how aggressive you are today." Clare smiled a sisterly smile in Sigrid's direction. She had always been a peacemaker.

"Sigrid does not shit," said Douglas. "Haven't you always secretly suspected it? Haven't you always wanted to meet a woman who was above that sort of thing?"

"What is your theory?" asked Joseph.

Sigrid considered. Since the results were flattering only to her, she quickly invented an alternative. There had been times when the group would have derived considerable sport from her little game, but today she felt her comrades were too fragile in spirit to play. Something was definitely bothering Douglas, and Joseph's ecstatic half-smiles were eerie, as if he had become a Moonie overnight. Even Clare seemed obscurely distressed and fidgety. Sigrid crushed out her cigarette and lowered her eyes a fraction. She touched the ends of her long hair, to show that she was feeling shy, and shrugged.

"Someone once told me it was obvious that I came from a blue-collar background," she lied. "He said I ate like a member of the working class trying to give myself airs."

"What an asshole *he* must have been," said Joseph loyally. "How can you take the opinion of a sadistic jerk so seriously?"

"You have perfectly lovely table manners," said Clare. "Do you know, Sig—that's the first insecure thing I've ever heard you say?"

"You're all so middle-class," said Sigrid. "You don't know what insecurity is, compared to me."

A soft snort from Douglas told her she'd overplayed her hand. When she met his eyes she saw, beneath the gleam of mockery, the I've-got-you-now, a subtle field of admiration.

"What was this scoundrel's name?" he asked. A challenge.

"Jesperson," she said, without a beat. "Charlie Jesperson." It was the name of her high-school chemistry teacher.

"Damn you, Lord Jesperson," Douglas spoke in a rich, melodramatic baritone, as if he were reading aloud from a work of fiction. "Damn you for your arrogance!" He pantomimed the act of composing on a typewriter. "Sigrid lifted a flushed face, full of defiance, and blinked back the tears threatening to spill from between her lashes. 'Why will you torment me this way? My people are as good and honorable as ever the Jesperson clan has been! How dare you insult me so?' Her sapphire eyes flashed defiantly as she tossed her mane of golden hair and confronted him with hatred. 'Ah, little Sigrid,' murmured the insolent man, his black eyes burning as they caressed her body, 'I do not hate you. Far from it.' Sigrid felt the hot pulsing of her blood. She was powerless to control the heaving of her white bosom, which threatened to overspill the confines of her tattered frock—" Douglas bowed in Sigrid's direction. "And et cetera," he concluded.

"How can you be such a *pig*?" Clare demanded. "Sometimes I

think you wouldn't know a moment of honesty if it grabbed you by the balls, Douglas."

"It's alright," said Sigrid. "Really, Clare. That was quite good, Douglas. You've got it down pat, except we don't say 'bosom' anymore. We've graduated to calling them breasts."

"But still they heave, no?"

"Oh yes," said Sigrid. "Always."

Joseph, or rather the new, Moonie-Joseph, smiled uneasily around the table. "I think I'll have another drink," he said.

"Me too," said Clare. When it was decided that each of them would have another drink, Douglas continuing with Scotch, Clare was dispatched to the bar to tell McCloy. Sigrid watched while Clare diffidently sidled up to the bar and conferred with Eugene. She parked one hip on a barstool and leaned toward him; the curve of her back and waist and hips viewed from this angle was rich and womanly. It struck Sigrid that Clare, Clare who worried about calories, might well have a white, heaving bosom.

Sigrid's own bosom was neat and meager. She seldom thought about it, but Douglas' scenario—herself as heroine—made her recall it now. Sigrid loved her body because it never gave her any trouble. It was more reliable than her typewriter, neither malfunctioning at awkward times nor requiring expensive servicing. It was asthetically pleasing—tidy and narrow—and looked well in clothes. It did not betray her with unexpected pains or unpleasant odors; the most trying ordeal it inflicted upon her was the inconvenience of her monthly menstruation, but even this was accomplished with a minimum of vexation. She was proud of the clockwork regularity of her menses and proud of the fact that she used exactly one box of Regular tampons each month. She knew that she could bear a child with relative ease, having done so at the age of nineteen, and was confident that no trace of this youthful indiscretion survived. If her bosom did not heave, neither did it droop.

37

Nevertheless, she felt somehow uneasy in her body while she waited for Clare to return, and she blamed it on Douglas. How clever of him—Douglas, of all people!—to have made a little play-let of her insincerity. Life still held surprises if Douglas Reville could detect her in a lie. She felt him at her side, an amused presence, while she listened to Joseph declare stimulants and writing incompatible.

"No crutches," he was saying earnestly. "It's got to come from inside, even the real crap, like Hawk. Somewhere, in all of us, is this—*cesspool,* if you like, of sentimentality. All the characters we invent are just ourselves, don't you think?"

Sigrid, who thought otherwise, merely smiled.

7

A Man's World

McCloy leafed through *Fiona's Folly,* sitting at the far end of the bar where his customers could not see what he was reading. Sigrid had presented it to him when she arrived, simply handing it over the bar on the way to the back room as if it were a sandwich he had ordered. It was inscribed to *Gene: who knows better than to read this. For your collection, with love. Sigrid Ericson. (Lucinda D'Arcy.)*

Sigrid was newer at writing these books than Clare, and possessed fewer pen names, but she wrote so quickly she was likely to catch up with the others before she hit thirty. She had told him she'd written *Fiona's Folly* in less than six weeks, and to McCloy, for whom writing was a tortuous process, this seemed a feat just short of miraculous.

He was becoming engrossed in a very nice description of the Scottish Highlands when Clare came to the bar. He was about to thrust the book beneath the bar, from reflex, before he realized there was no need. Clare sat on the stool opposite him and inclined toward him. There was something dreamy in her movements; he reckoned it was the effects of the Irish whiskey added to her usual Bloody Marys. He asked what he could do for her. "Coffee for anyone?"

"Why, Gene," she said. "You're reading Sigrid's book!"

She spoke with such amazement McCloy immediately wished he had put it out of sight. To obscure his embarrassment, he began to read from the passage about the Highlands out loud. His reading glasses were playing him up again, and he was obliged to hold *Fiona's Folly* at some distance from his face.

"It was a fine summer's day," he read, "and in the glen the winds blew sweetly, carrying the scent of fresh, wild grasses to Fiona. On the high purple slopes the clouds cast shadows as they scudded across the high arc of the blue sky, and Fiona felt the summer enter into her, filling her with joy."

He saw, farther down on the page, the word "breast" looming up, and halted. "That's what I call poetic," he said to Clare. "It's fine writing."

"I'll tell Sig," said Clare. "She'll be pleased."

There was a tautness in Clare's voice that warned him that some gallantry was required here. "It reminds me of some of the descriptions in your books. Take the one that had the romance with the pirate and the red-haired girl, Clare."

"*Fortune's Strumpet.* One of my worst, Gene."

"Well, that may be, Clare, but I can recall some first-rate descriptions of the sea in that one. Especially when they had the big storm in the Caribbean."

"Thank you, Gene." Her voice softened and she smiled on him so tenderly he was relieved when she gave the drink order. The truth was that he was deeply embarrassed by the sort of book Clare and Sigrid wrote so effortlessly. One saw such books in the supermarkets and train stations, of course, but a man would go his whole life without looking into them because they were intended only for women. He quite enjoyed dipping into the novels of Joseph and Douglas. They dealt with sex in a straightforward, manly way McCloy could recognize as appropriate. A fellow would meet a sexy girl and be attracted by her. There was always some byplay before they could get together, but nothing like the stuff you encountered in the girls' books. When Hawk, for example, bedded a sexy bit of stuff, it was always quite enjoyable for both parties. A little raw for his taste, sometimes, but not near as bad as the hard-core kind of book.

He told Clare to go back, he would bring the drinks. She had been hovering, as if she expected to help him. If they had been alone he might have humored her, but Jimmy and the other two still sat at the bar, rather stuporous by now, and it would not do to relax the rules in his own establishment in front of them.

He took special pains with her Bloody Mary, dashing in the extra Tabasco she liked, and made Sigrid's milder. Joseph's beer he drew with exquisite care, and splashed more than a shot of Dewar's into Douglas' glass. No, he thought, arranging the drinks on a tray, it was not the eternally heaving breasts and hot thighs of the women in books like *Fiona* that bothered him—these were standard issue and also appeared in the men's novels—but rather the circumstances that triggered the pulsing, heaving, burning, throbbing, fiery, ecstatic, volcanic, galvanic, *lunatic* responses of the ladies. And then, if they were so mightily pleased by the doings Clare and Sigrid had contrived for them, why did they go all coy and neurotic and desert (sometimes for hundreds of pages) the men who had so satisfied them?

Was it because they had been raped? McCloy could understand a woman's repugnance for her rapist, but Clare's and Sigrid's women wanted to be raped. It was as clear as anything; face it, they were asking for it.

Eugene carried the drinks to the back room, composing his face in an impassive mask to conceal from them what it was he had been pondering.

"Won't you sit down with us, Gene?" Joseph's request came unexpectedly. The lad, cowboy boots and earphones notwithstanding, seemed in trouble. McCloy could read the signs. Joseph was feeling the need of an ally, or witness. Eugene's heart went out to him, although the nature of Joe's distress was unknown to him. Was he still grieving over the feckless wife? Joseph, although far too old to fit the bill, called up McCloy's paternal instincts.

"Can't at the moment," he said. "Cook's just leaving."

"I guess I'll go now," said Jaime the cook, as he did each afternoon at this time. "There's coffee, if they want any." Jimmy and one of the other old men were stirring feebly on their stools, preparing to leave in Jaime's wake. They had it all figured out by now: if they drank only until the cook's departure they could afford to return in the evening. By judiciously husbanding their drinks, and in the certain knowledge of having several on the house, they managed to spend eight hours a day in Eugene's.

McCloy watched stiff fingers buttoning up, pulling caps lower, resisting the impulse to pocket the loose change on the counter. "I might look in tonight," said Jimmy, before he shuffled to the door.

"You do that, now," said McCloy. He watched the two men, outside on the sleeted pavement, turn in the direction of the hotel where they lived just off Amsterdam. They did not speak, any more than they did when they sat apart at the bar. The light was fading fast for a midafternoon in March. The world observed from the window seemed bleak and without promise. McCloy checked to see that his remaining customer lacked nothing, and then returned to his perch at the end of the bar and *Fiona's Folly*.

Here, to prove his point, was Fiona's first sexual encounter with Laird Bruce of the Glen. She had come to beg for mercy for her little brother Angus, who had been caught poaching rabbits on Bruce land. He scanned the long description of the way her tattered garments clung to the various protuberances of her body and skipped over the dialogue. He ignored the loving passages about Laird Bruce's well-muscled thighs—Christ, who wanted to read about another man's legs?—and got to the gist of things. The arrogant Laird promised to spare Angus a flogging if Fiona would give him a kiss. Tears streaming down her face, Fiona complied, which set up the heaving, pulsing mechanism he had noted earlier. Fiona, it seemed, was angry because she liked the kiss, and so she raked her nails over the man's face until the blood ran. Quite naturally, this enraged Laird Bruce, who raped her to teach her a lesson.

Certainly, thought McCloy, Laird Bruce had no right to ravish the girl for scratching him, but look how much Fiona liked it! In the course of one paragraph, the "ripping, searing agony" she felt as he battered his way into her virginal body became "a bright, fiery core of pleasure which spread to every fiber of her being, threatening to consume her in its white heat."

He turned the page, and here was Fiona raking her lover's flesh again, this time his back, of course, and making a great deal of noise. Page 35, it was. Shortly after the "crashing tidal wave of pleasure" had subsided, she was telling Laird Bruce how much she hated him. "I would sooner mate with the Devil than look on your hateful face again" was the way she put it.

McCloy riffled through the book now, halting only occasionally to read some hot scenes involving the Laird and a girl called Molly MacGregor. Fiona married, achieved a lesser degree of fiber-consuming heat with her husband, was raped by several other men, enjoying it less than she had that first time. Finally, on page 321, Laird Bruce appeared again. Fiona's husband had died and she was free to admit that she had never loved anyone the way she loved the man she'd hated on page 35. The novel concluded with what McCloy could only think of as a mutual rape, Fiona's hands sliding up inside the Laird's kilts toward "the rock of his manhood."

On the very last page was a little printed questionnaire. *What rating would you give* Fiona's Folly? was the first question. Mentally, he checked off *excellent,* out of loyalty to Sigrid. *What prompted you to buy this book?* Certainly not the cover, which was one of the choices offered. He would have to check *other* and write in that it was a gift. The questionnaire also sought his age group, *35–45,* and wanted to know if the love scenes were *too explicit, not explicit enough,* or *just right*. What would he say, if he were obliged to answer these questions?

"In my humble opinion," he might write, "explicitness is not the issue. You are fooling people about the act of sex. You are being explicit about things that do not exist."

McCloy closed the book, slipped it under the counter, and removed his reading glasses. The back room sprang into sharp focus, and he saw that his hacks appeared to be having a small argument. Voices were not raised, but Joseph was frowning, Douglas gesticulating, and the line of Clare's back seemed tense. Only Sigrid seemed detached. She picked up her glass and held it to her lips, as if to hide a smile. He looked at the slender fingers clutching the thick stem and thought of how her fingernails were bitten to the quick. Characteristically, she had done an even job on them, but the mutilated nails were the one thing about her that did not speak of control and discipline.

You noticed hands, tending bar. Clare's were unpredictable. Sometimes all ten nails were long and carefully shaped, polished in a blaze of glamorous color; other times they were broken and split and Clare would examine them, holding her hand out that way all women did, and sigh. She had explained that a writer could never hope to have consistantly nice nails unless she wrote in longhand and hired a typist. "Occupational hazard," she said.

Oh, Clare. Oh, Sigrid. Soldiers of fortune in a man's world, breaking their nails to churn out steamy tales for the edification of women they would never know but whom they might, themselves, become in time—what was there in the universe to protect them?

Did they think, secretly, that a powerful man with steely thighs and manhood like a rock would come to ravish them and carry them away from their typewriters? Clare had been married to a man she referred to always as the Leech, while Sigrid, so much younger, seemed immaculate as a nun. If he didn't know better, he might assume she was a virgin, but there were no virgins under thirty any more.

He emptied the heaping ashtray in front of his last remaining cloth cap and poured himself a shot of Paddy's. It was not the drink he wanted, but the warmth.

"Where's the joke?" asked his customer. The man had seen the involuntary twitch of the lips that had accompanied Eugene's vivid mental image. McCloy had no joke to offer him and was caught out feeling guilty. He conversed with him on the subject of horses—one eye on his hacks—for some time by way of compensation.

What he had been thinking when his lips stretched in that mirthless smile was this: if Laird Bruce and Sigrid confronted each other this very night, there would be no way for them to get together. She had no fingernails with which to rake his face or back.

On such small points, it seemed, hung whole destinies.

8

Reviews to Kill For

Astoundingly, Mr. Reville is the author of some twenty books, unheralded and unsung, whose themes have embraced the major issues of the last two decades with a compassion and fidelity that leaves this reviewer awed, humbled, and angry at a world which allows the talents of such a man as Douglas Reville to languish in obscurity.

Having begun the argument, Douglas tired of it first and left Sigrid and Joseph to slug it out, with Clare as mediator. He retired into the world of his favorite new pastime, inventing, then perfecting, reviews he would like to read in *The New York Times*. "Semi-obscurity" would be better, he thought. He didn't wish to be portrayed as a complete dud. The particular review he had been imagining was an old friend; thus Douglas could amuse himself with it and still be alert enough to thrust his oar into the conversation if need be.

"I'm not simpleminded, you know," Joseph was saying. "I'm not trying to suggest that everything in a novel is autobiographical. That's what my dimmer students used to think. Back when I was teaching, it used to drive me crazy, they'd raise their hands and insist that Joyce was Jewish. Or they'd write papers about the author as if he were the character in the novel assigned.

"I'll never forget—I think I saved this one—a kid wrote: 'The pessimistic outlook of Ibsen's *Ghosts* was certainly due to the syphilis from which the author suffered at the time.'"

"Aren't you glad you weren't granted tenure?" said Clare.

"Oh, this opens up wonderful possibilities," said Sigrid. "'The pessimistic outlook of much of Flannery O'Connor's fiction is certainly due to the wooden leg she wore while writing it.'"

"'Victor Hugo's pessimism was undoubtedly the product of his terrible deformity,'" announced Clare.

"Or," said Sigrid, delighted by the game, "you could turn it around. How about: 'The horrible fate of Dorian Gray was assuredly prompted by Oscar Wilde's disgust at the decadence he encountered while an undergraduate at Oxford'?"

"My point," said Joseph with a weary smile, "is getting obscured here. I was only saying that every character I write is somehow—*me.* Men, women, children—heroic, weak, innocent—all *me.* Idealized me, debased me, only, sometimes, fractionally me, but still *me.* How can it be different?"

"Hawk is you?" Clare spoke smartly, as if she were the moderator of a panel discussion. "Hawk's instincts, Joe? Are they your own? Idealized, of course, and made all nice and one-dimensional—are they yours?"

"Of course. Hawk is just a dumber, braver, handsomer version of Joe Auerbach if he had been born thirty years earlier to a patriotic WASP family in Indianapolis."

Reville's failure to achieve a measure of recognition in his native land speaks not for any failure on the author's part, but for the relentless commercialism of current publishing practices. . . .

"What about the SS officer who likes to break fingers by slamming drawers on them?" said Clare. "Is he a sadistic version of Joe

Auerbach if he had been born to a patriotic Nazi family in Hamburg?"

"You could say that." Joseph's tone was defiant. "Klaus' inner motivations—he's brutal because he's afraid of appearing weak—are probably similar to mine. If I were a sadist."

"Or a Nazi," said Sigrid.

"Oh, come *on!* You're all being deliberately obtuse." He turned on Clare first. "When you write a rape scene in one of your novels, the heroine's responses are yours, in some sense. Even though you, Clare, would not enjoy being raped, whatever the heroine finds to enjoy is something you would enjoy in the act of lovemaking."

Clare and Sigrid burst into laughter on cue.

"It's just a *formula,* Joe," said Clare.

"It's not what *we'd* like," said Sigrid, "it's what the ladies who read those books like. Or think they'd like."

> *Even in such formulaic writing as his "Slattery" detective series, Reville displays an uncommon gift for capturing the essence of his New York low-lifes in lean, deftly crafted prose that is reminiscent of Raymond Chandler at the height of his powers.*

"Come on, Douglas," said Joseph. "Help me out here."

"What I think," said Douglas, "is that this discussion is unbelievably boring and should be terminated at once." Joseph's puppy eyes actually misted over with pain at this betrayal, but he knew the rules.

"Yeah," he said. "I guess I was getting pretty sophomoric there. *Mea culpa.*"

"Ego te absolvum," said Douglas. He realized he had spoken more loudly than he'd meant to because Eugene looked up from his perch with mild alarm. Eugene wasn't the only one looking at him—Clare and Sigrid turned reproachful eyes in his direction.

"You're rather brutal today," said Clare. "Something must be troubling you."

He felt the muscle in his cheek jump. Control yourself, he thought; control must be maintained. You aren't a bad fellow, really—the little rush of pleasure you get from shutting Joe up, the power and pleasure that always accompanies meanness, they're replaced almost instantly by pity, followed by guilt, followed by the need to atone. You must tell an amusing story now, and everyone will love you again.

He had an amusing story at the ready, a legitimate, timely tale they would all enjoy, but he was not in the mood to tell it. He thought a trip to the men's room might restore his social instincts, and so he smiled in a conciliatory way and went off sheepishly, he hoped, to relieve himself.

> *Other comparisons come to mind in assessing Reville's fiction, but the reviewer does not mean to imply that the author is in any way derivative. His is a unique sensibility, capable of endowing Samantha, heroine of the pulp classic "Bride of the Cherokee," with a lustiness worthy of Fielding or Smollett, together with a spiritual inner life George Eliot herself would not have scorned to chronicle. . . .*

No, that was going too far. Not George Eliot. Mary McCarthy?

HARNESS SORROW.

Douglas saw it as he was zipping up and wondered if Joseph could have written it on his last trip to the men's room. It was exactly the sort of thing poor Joey would write, if he was drunk enough. His conviction that Joseph was secretly plotting a serious work returned, and he felt numb with pity. He searched in the pockets of his Harris tweed for a pen, sensing the importance of blotting out the graffito, but his fingers felt large and incapable. He encountered Sigrid's book and his wallet and a packet of tissues purchased when he had suffered from a cold, but nothing with which to write. His hands made the tour several times with dumb incredulity. He saw himself with a lack of charity: a middle-aged man standing at a urinal, conducting a body-search so that he might eradicate two words scrawled on a shit-house wall by a younger man who was still hopeful. Furthermore, the middle-aged man, once capable of downing vast quantities of drink without ill effect, was tolerably drunk in the middle of the afternoon on three whiskies. His step as he turned from the urinal toward the washbasin was slightly unsteady. He avoided his image in the mirror.

Considering Reville's lack of recognition—he has never been reviewed in any major publication to this writer's knowledge—it would scarcely be surprising to detect a note of bitterness in his writing. This is not the case. His compassion for his characters seems limitless; perhaps it would not be amiss to suggest that Douglas Reville has harnessed the sorrow he must feel in the face of the publishing world's indifference and made it work for him. . . .

In the corridor, he found McCloy approaching with a roll of paper toweling beneath his arm. They sidled past one another with many smiles and gestures of masculine bonhomie. Just when he thought Eugene would dissappear into the men's room, McCloy detained him in that mysterious, Irish way he had of commanding one's attention by inactivity.

"Douglas," he murmured. "There's something I've been meaning to ask you." The lowered voice, the slightly shifty look in McCloy's eyes suggested that the point in question might turn out to be an embarrassing one. Douglas leaned against the wall, waiting, and the silence lengthened. Was Gene going to elicit his support in a campaign to bed Clare or Sigrid? Or did he intend to ask if Douglas was the author of HARNESS SORROW and reprove him for marring the walls of his lavatory?

"Those books the girls write," said Gene furtively, "with all the carrying on—is there a rule at the publishing places about the raping?" He studied his roll of toweling and gave a little apologetic laugh. "What I mean—do the heroines *have* to be raped?"

Stranger and stranger, thought Douglas. McCloy might object to the rapes on moral grounds, or his interest might be prurient. "It's not exactly a rule, Gene. More like a convention." He remembered the one time he had turned his hand to a bodice-ripper, his *Bride of the Cherokee.* Good royalties, he recalled, but not an experience he'd want to repeat. He had felt strangely unmanned, writing from a woman's point of view. "Yes," he assured McCloy, "definitely a convention."

"You wonder why," said McCloy.

"The heroines are good girls, Gene. Back in those days, good girls didn't race you to the sack, so in order to get some sex in, you've got to get 'em raped. That way they can enjoy it without guilt. It isn't their fault if some pirate ties them to the mast and slips it to them—see what I mean?"

McCloy looked relieved. "Yes, it makes sense." He nodded several times, as if they had been discussing a fine point of law, tapped Douglas' arm lightly by way of thanks, and continued on his way. Douglas stared after him. At the door of the men's room McCloy paused, then turned back.

"I was only thinking of the girls," he said softly. "Wondering if it was good for them to be writing about rape all the time."

"Clare and Sigrid could write a rape scene in their sleep by now. Don't worry about them."

"Not so long as I know it's a convention," said McCloy.

Douglas returned to the table, nurturing his secret amusement at

Gene's concern. He wasn't sure whether he'd tell Clare and Sigrid or not.

> *Of course "Bride of the Cherokee" is marred by the obligatory sex scenes which occur with the dreary regularity necessary to the genre, but even here Reville has succeeded in . . .*

No.

> *Even the obligatory, steamy sex scenes are conveyed with integrity and a realistic, if dark, passion, which transcends the genre utterly. This reviewer, at least, was reminded of John Updike.*

Why not?

9

Killing Off Eileen

"How about influenza?" said Clare. "The epidemic of 1918?"

"A little too late," said Douglas.

"Accidental drowning? Or suicide! Have her drown herself."

"It can't be anything that dramatic, because that would influence later generations. If she commits suicide it's bound to have an effect on her children."

"Douglas is right," said Sigrid. "A heart attack is best."

"At the age of thirty-eight?" Clare's own age.

"It's been known to happen. Give her a rheumatic heart."

"Pneumonia's always believable," Joseph said, "before penicillin was invented."

They were discussing Douglas' latest dilemma, introduced, Joseph knew, to distract them all from his earlier churlishness. Douglas had asked their advice on how best to kill off Eileen Hennessy, a character in his current book. Douglas had not planned to end her life, originally, and was miffed that he was now obliged to do so.

Douglas was writing Volume III of a family saga (or "generational," as they were called in the trade), spanning five generations of the family Hennessy. The Hennessys were an immigrant clan of indigent Irish peasantry who came to America in steerage and suffered, strived, brawled, connived, clawed, plotted, and fucked their way to success. They were exactly like the feisty immigrants in *The Lundquists* —a Swedish family saga to which Clare had once contributed a volume—only Irish. Joseph could easily write the blurb:

> *From the famine-ravaged villages of Galway, the teeming slums of Dublin—they blazed a path of Freedom to the green shores of the New World! In this brawling, passionate tale of greed, lust, courage, and conviction,* THE HENNESSYS *live the glory and the tragedy, the heartbreak and the epic grandeur, of the American Dream!*

The only thing that made *The Hennessys* different from a dozen other generationals was that all five volumes were being written simultaneously by five different writers. Douglas' problem was a perfect example of the irritating, trivial kind of snags a writer was always encountering in hack work. Joseph was fully in sympathy; any resentment he had felt at Douglas' high-handed treatment was gone, washed away by the endearingly humble way in which he had sought their advice in the matter of Eileen Hennessy's demise.

"All five of us have Xeroxed copies of the family tree," he had explained. "The only time we met we exchanged outlines and got everything squared away neatly—births, marriages, deaths. Everything accounted for. Eileen Hennessy, she's the mother of Deirdre, my main female, is a perfectly nice woman, about thirty-eight, former beauty now slightly worn from childbearing. She had her star turn in Volume Two. In my book she's a doting mother settling in for a cozy middle age." Douglas had lifted his glass to Clare. "Women aged faster back then," he said.

"Anyway, I hit page two hundred last night and thought I'd better phone the guy who's doing Volume Four just to make sure we're in synch. Sure enough, all the main characters are where I need them to be in his book. Deirdre is having an affair with a rogue priest, Liam is about to get in with the IRA, and Finbar is running for the US Senate. Fine. Then I ask about Eileen—whether she's still in Boston or maybe down in New York, keeping an eye on Deirdre, who's run off with Father O'Toole—and there's this—silence. 'Eileen?' the guy says finally. 'Who's that?'

"'She's Deirdre's *mother,*' I tell him, not believing my ears. More silence, then the riffling of papers at the other end. 'Not in *my* book,' he says. 'I thought she was dead.' I asked him what the hell I was supposed to do about that, kind of indignant by this time. 'Kill her off,' he said. He was apologetic, but it was the only solution he could think of. Kill her off."

Everyone had laughed, as Douglas had intended them to do, and set about inventing ways for Eileen Hennessy to meet her end before 1916.

"There's always the *Titanic,*" Clare said.

"What would a woman like Eileen be doing on the *Titanic?* Anyway, it's been done too many times before."

"Why should you be the one to change things?" Sigrid's tone was amused but indignant. "That man had the same charts you did. He was supposed to know Eileen was still in the running. Make him write her in."

"The son of a bitch has already finished," said Douglas. "He handed it in three days ago."

Joseph laughed with the rest of them, but beneath the glow of comradely good feeling the Tuesday lunches always inspired in him, he felt the danger signals. Here came a little puff of sadness, Vivvy-related sadness, because Douglas' story was exactly the sort of thing he used to bring home to her. He would ride the subway back to Brooklyn, his mood nearly euphoric when he had harvested material for her amusement.

How she had loved to hear about the trials and peculiar problems of the hacks! "Oh, stop!" she would cry, rolling about on their quilted bed as if in the throes of some sadomasochistic experiment,

"I can't *stand* it! You're making it *up*!" She had become the hit of her Wall Street law firm, relating these anecdotes to awed secretaries and indulgent junior partners. A *raconteur*.

In those days he had felt himself to be a kind of hero—a free lance in a tournament of the absurd, jousting with publishers and packagers and wily agents, all for the entertainment and sustenance of his lady.

"What is Liam to Eileen? What relationship?" Stern Sigrid, now smoking her second cigarette, posed the question importantly.

"Son."

"Well, Liam could get his mother killed, accidentally, as a result of his revolutionary activities. If no one ever knew, even Liam, you'd have a dramatically fulfilling death and a very moving situation." Sigrid held her hands up, as if to frame a cinematic shot. "There's Eileen, breathing her last, praying for her children with her last breaths as the life's blood runs from her, never knowing that the son she bore in love and agony was the instrument of her own death!"

Joseph's sadness escalated from a puff of sentiment to a steady little breeze, menacing now. Sigrid's earnest scenario was so much the sort of thing Vivvy had enjoyed inventing, imagining she was helping him in his work. Of course, Vivvy was not nearly so skilled as Sig; her technique was amateurish, her language not that of pulp fiction, but what effort she had expended in trying to help him write his way out of awkward situations!

It was she who had suggested some love interest for Trudy, Hawk's wife. If Trudy could be tempted in the direction of an adulterous affair, Vivvy pointed out, then the reader would grant Hawk a greater share of leniency when *he* strayed, which worked out to two times per book. Joseph had been delighted, indulgent. It had certainly never occurred to him to be jealous at the surprisingly lubricious quality of his wife's inventions. She was only helping him.

What did occur to Joseph these days, with a tormenting regularity, was that he had been a fool. He had ignored certain clearly erected signposts, denoting Vivvy's dissatisfaction, in the belief that her new feverish imagination was the natural by-product of being married to a writer. He had been sure that her disappointment, on finding that he would not be reviewed in the *Times,* was merely a wifely statement of solidarity and loyalty. Her chagrin at the amount of his royalty checks he found adorably naive. On the night when she had blanched to discover that his first earning statement for one of the Hawk books placed him in the packager's debt (although not really, as he had assured her), she wept. Fine sex had ensued, informed by Joseph's conviction that Vivvy's tears were a positive proof of her belief in him, her rage at a world that did not grant him the credit he was due.

He knew now that Vivvy had wept because she was losing faith in him. He was bringing her no nearer to the time when she might quit the Wall Street law firm, no nearer to an apartment in Manhattan, drinks at Elaine's, publication parties at the Tavern on the Green. Part of her pleasure in bed that night, despite the tears, might well have come from making a decision.

Joseph reached back and thrust his arms into the sleeves of his jacket, settling it about himself as unobtrusively as possible. There was an instant flurry of protest from the others, who thought he was planning to leave. He explained that he was merely cold, invented a mysterious draft that affected only the place where he was seated. Douglas, who was sweating, lifted an eyebrow.

"I still think Joe's idea is best," said Clare. "Pneumonia. It's clean and credible."

What if Vivvy had decided that very night to leave him? She could have been thinking of the stock analyst she eventually ran off with even as she lay in Joseph's arms; at the moment of orgasm she might have hit upon the plan with the U-Haul.

Joseph excused himself and went off in the direction of the men's room. His Walkman nuzzled at his fingertips when he thrust a hand in his pocket. It was almost as comforting as the feel of a beloved dog's muzzle poking the distressed master's palm.

Alone in the men's room, he leaned against the wall to steady himself. Remarkable, he thought, what pain could be experienced through the simple expedient of picturing oneself as a fool. He had never seen the stock analyst, whose name was Matthew, and knew only that his earning powers were very adult, although he was a year younger than Joseph. He thought Vivvy and Matthew were living together in Manhattan now. At first there had been telephone conversations, painful yet somehow reassuring, but gradually they ceased. Once, in January, prompted by a blizzard of the sort they both had loved, he had called her at the law firm. He had had a vague notion on that day, an almost psychic feeling that Vivvy was yearning toward him, regretting her flight. An unfamiliar voice informed him that Vivian Auerbach had left the firm's employ a month before.

Joseph extracted the Schubert tape and inserted what he believed to be a cassette of *Nashville Skyline.* He placed the little earphones on his head and pushed the button, waiting for music to come and displace his grief. Instead of Dylan's twanging, good-humored voice, he heard the beginning of the tape he had specially recorded to help him write his real novel. In his haste on leaving the apartment, he had grabbed it by mistake.

Into Joseph's ears and whole being streamed the pure, heartbreaking sounds of Vivaldi's "Winter" section of the *Four Seasons.* It was the very music he used to stir his sorrow at the typewriter, for he associated it so strongly with Vivvy, the two had now become inseparable in his mind. The mechanism that worked so well in harnessing his sorrow to serve his art was fatal in a men's room, and Joseph felt tears spill from his eyes at the first pizzicato violin. He saw his face reflected in the mirror: the face of a foolish, self-indulgent man, crumpled and uncomely in grief. This made him cry harder.

He turned the machine off and replaced it in his pocket. Obediently, the tears slackened and became manageable. He splashed cold water on his face and scrubbed it dry with harsh paper toweling, newly installed by Eugene.

When he returned to the table, the others were looking pleased.

"We killed her off," said Sigrid. "Eileen is stung by a bee at a garden party."

"She happens to be one of the unfortunate few who are fatally allergic," said Clare.

"Eileen Hennessy, dead at thirty-eight, of bee-bite," said Douglas.

Joseph removed his jacket again and looked around at his clever friends. "RIP," he said. "Poor lady."

They drank a toast to Eileen Hennessy and then, noticing their nearly empty glasses, decided to have another round.

10

Gentrification

Maxine from the hosiery store up the block surprised McCloy by coming in at three-thirty for a drink. She occasionally dropped by at lunchtime, but he had never known her to enter his place at any other time.

"I don't know," she said, as if McCloy had demanded her to explain her presence. "I've never understood what people saw in drinking, if you'll pardon me for saying so, but there must be something to it. It makes millions of people happy, doesn't it?"

Eugene thought of Nora, who was likely to be on her tenth gin and cranberry juice by now. "You could say that," he conceded.

"Something just came over me today. I was feeling, well, a little down to begin with, and then the whole day went"—she spread her hands, flashing the long, lacquered nails of which she was so proud—"ka-flooey! A whole shipment of the queen-sized panty hose turned out to be mismarked, and then some crazy woman came in and said she'd left her credit card and why hadn't we notified her? I said, 'I can assure you, madam, that no lost credit cards have been found here,' but I could tell she wouldn't believe me."

"Yes, that's trying," said McCloy. "It's very trying, not to be believed."

"Then I couldn't go out to lunch, and when Roseanne brought me my sandwich from the deli it was not what I had ordered. It was tongue instead of corned beef, and I have never liked tongue."

"Nor have I, come to think of it."

"It used to be, at the deli, that you could trust the countermen. Not any more. It's been bought out, you know, and they're going for the younger crowd. They'll do it slowly, wean away all the old customers, and next thing you know there'll be nothing but health-food salads and those long loaves of bread you see in travel ads for France. The whole block is going down, Mr. McCloy. We're the last holdouts—my shop and your place. I wonder how long we can last."

"People will always need stockings," said McCloy gallantly.

Maxine touched her towering coiffure of flame-red hair and smiled sadly. "Don't bet on it," she said.

"What can I get you, Mrs. Passle? It does seem to me you need cheering up."

"It's such a *depressing* day, isn't it? Weather affects people's moods—I read that somewhere. You're nice and snug here, though. Your place was the only one I'd dare go into at this hour. I feel safe here, Mr. McCloy. If I was to waltz into that new place up the block—the one with all those plants in the window—they'd treat me like dirt. Yes, like dirt. All those young men wearing eye makeup, they're supposed to be so gentle on account of their feminine personalities, let me tell you—they're meaner than real men! They snicker behind your back. Sometimes to your face. They don't care."

McCloy began to feel alarm. It seemed to him that Maxine was on the verge of some momentous breaking apart—he was conversant with the signs—and he was torn between the sympathy he felt for her and the ardent wish that she not disintegrate in his establishment. Since it seemed clear that she would not be capable of ordering a drink, he cast about for the perfect treat to set before her. What would please a sixtyish woman, fond of bright colors and garish trouser-suits; what would distract her from the distressing conviction, no doubt true, that she and her hosiery shop had outlived their time?

"I haven't told you the strangest thing," she said, opening her bag and extracting the cigarettes that had turned her voice from the treble of youth to a sort of rakish bass. "One of those mousy dancers came in for a pair of leotards. She looked like skim milk, if you can appreciate what I mean. When I was writing up the sales slip I made a comment about the weather. I said it was a depressing day, more the kind of day you'd expect in winter. You know what she said?"

Maxine bent toward him, cigarette between her lips. McCloy noticed where her crimson lipstick had begun to congeal at the corners of her mouth. He lit her cigarette and watched while she inhaled mournfully. When the smoke had been expelled she said, "The Ides of March."

"Excuse me?"

"That's what the girl told me. The day is depressing because it's the Ides of March. I suppose it has something to do with astrology. That's what all the young people are worshiping now—the stars."

McCloy turned away and began to concoct a drink for her, since she had still not expressed a preference. In the mirror over the bar he saw the reflection of his hacks. He had long since taken their plates away and they sat with fresh drinks, talking quietly. Now and again some of their earlier animation re-emerged, but they seemed languid and a little dispirited. It was the effect of the unusual number of drinks, he knew. Each of them had reached the stage when motor skills were slightly impaired, although they were far from drunk. Another round and they would turn raucous. That was the first of the last three stages of heavy drinking: from bellicose to lachrymose to comatose, as Nora would have it. He hoped they would quit now. It unsettled him to see his writers behaving like regular bar customers.

"Two more nights and you'll be busy," Maxine said. "I imagine I wouldn't even know the place then." Her eyes widened as he set the drink before her. "Why, Mr. McCloy—it's gorgeous! What is it?"

"It's called a grasshopper."

"It seems a shame to drink it," she said. She lifted the little glass and studied the bright green liquid, squinting. "I don't want to know what's in this grasshopper thing, that would ruin it. I'll just pretend it's medicine and you're the doctor." She sipped at it timidly. "Very tasty, too. Like candy."

By rights, McCloy thought, Joseph should be least affected, drinking only beer, but it was Sigrid who seemed soberest. Sometimes those little lean women, built like whippets, could put the stuff away like stevedores. Douglas was beginning to resemble a melting candle, while Clare was flushed and glittering.

"A hosiery shop closed last week further down Broadway, the Jolie Madame," said Maxine. "They raised their lease by two hundred percent, the greedy so-and-sos. Roseanne tells me the new owners are going to turn it into a cheese shop. Where's the sense in that? You want cheese, you can get it at the supermarket."

McCloy, whose barber had been forced to leave to make way for a concern that sold nothing but bathroom soaps, smiled.

"We're being gentrified," he said. "That's what they call it. Gentrification."

"Ka-flooey," said Maxine. "It's all going ka-flooey." She consulted her watch and frowned, then downed the remainder of her grasshopper quickly. "That was delicious," she told McCloy. "I needed a lift." She brought out her wallet, a large mock-alligator affair, but McCloy assured her the drink was his.

"We have to stand together against gentrification," he said. "The pleasure was mine."

Maxine unearthed a tube of Life Savers from her purse and popped one in her mouth to conceal the fragrance of her unaccustomed afternoon vice. As she was thanking McCloy, a commotion arose from the back room. Douglas' voice was heard to ask in positively warlike tones:

"How many reviews? Let's see a show of hands! How many fucking *reviews?*"

"Who are those people?" Maxine swiveled on her seat at the sound of the dangerous voice. Her posture was alert, her expression that of a passenger who has encountered terrorists in the airport lounge.

"They come here every other Tuesday," said Eugene. "For lunch."

"But it's nearly a quarter to four! Why are they eating lunch at three forty-five?"

"They're writers," said Eugene.

"So writers eat lunch later than other people?"

"I am calling for a fucking show of *hands!*" Douglas shouted.

"What do they write?" Maxine said darkly. "They look like no-goods to me, never mind what they sound like."

"Well, books," said Eugene. "Novels. That sort of thing."

Maxine laughed then, the green froth on her upper lip looking quite festive in contrast to the scarlet lipstick. In laughing she revealed several moldering molars of a bluish cast, but McCloy saw her at that moment as she might have been some thirty years earlier; in her honest mirth, Maxine appeared quite youthful and carefree—rapture had been liberated by the suggestion that there were people living on the earth more useless and antiquated than she.

"*Writers,*" she whispered. "Don't they have anything better to do?"

11

Fine Instincts

Clare's life thus far, for thirty-eight years or so, can be viewed two ways. To the people with whom she grew up, it would seem quite daring; thrilling, even. Except for two members of her high school graduating class in Homeport, Oregon—one of whom was killed in a mass murder, one who became a composer well-known in Moog synthesizer circles—Clare is the most celebrated. To people who live in faster circles of society, her life would seem a rather small affair, acceptable, but lived at the lower rungs of what is considered exciting.

Clare has had two careers and two husbands. She is widely traveled and has had affairs with minor celebrities, as well as with unknown individuals. Sometimes, when she doubts the jauntiness of the swath she has cut through her nearly two score years in life, she lists her accomplishments as if in preparation for an autobiography to be read by her peers in Homeport.

As in an autobiography, a section for photos has been reserved. When Clare lacks the necessary photo (or finds the one at hand unflattering), she supplies imaginary ones. It is a pastime she finds especially useful when she is trying to go to sleep. Instead of counting sheep, Clare hunts for the perfect photograph with which to bridge the gap between her career as actress and her career as writer, or searches for an image appropriate to her current state in life. Usually, she convinces herself. She is an interesting person, has had an eventful life. Only occasionally does she harbor an upsetting conviction—a suspicion, really—that her adventures have not been unusual enough or her achievements substantial enough to lift her above the commonplace.

"Sometimes," she says to the group, "I regret not having had any children."

"Oh Christ, not you, too." Douglas speaks wearily, as if he had been confronted with dozens of women all voicing the same regret. "That's passé, sweetheart. That went out last decade—all those feminists picking some poor bastard for his good genes and then naming the kid Daughter Motherschild or whatever."

Clare is suddenly tired of Douglas' bullying ways, even though she knows he is secretly as fragile as an egg. His calling for a show of hands, for example, was just another way of making them all realize how unimportant they were. Here they were, calling themselves writers, yet not a one of them had ever been recognized in print. Not where it counted. Douglas would not allow inky paragraphs breathlessly extolling the virtues of a bodice-ripper in the *Romance Times,* or the praise for Joseph's Hawk once encountered in a magazine put out for would-be mercenaries. She turns on Douglas now, with all the wrath she can summon.

"I did not say I wanted to conduct a ludicrous experiment, Douglas. It was not my intention to imply that I longed for a Clareschild who would be subjected to infusions of feminist literature along with its mother's milk. I merely said I *sometimes* regretted not having any children. I did not make the statement to give you an opportunity to hold me up to ridicule; in fact, I wasn't eager for your reaction at all. You must not make the mistake of replying to everything that's said. Learn to be silent occasionally, Douglas."

"Yes, *ma'am!*" says Douglas, pretending to cower beneath her words. He throws his tweedy arms up to protect himself and smiles engagingly, but Clare has seen the rogue muscle twitch furiously at her assault and knows she has wounded him.

"Excellent advice," says Sigrid.

Joseph, too, is cowering, although it takes a practiced eye to see it. All afternoon, Clare thinks, he has reminded her of a man who has just undergone major surgery and fears his stitches will open. Now he looks as if he fears something more direct—an attack by enraged women who will accuse him of male crimes. She smiles at Joey, wanting to reassure him, and feels the potent force of her female allure rushing across the table toward him and signaling that which she does not intend.

"I have three children, as you know," says Douglas. "I see them once a year, in rotation. My son, the oldest, calls me Mr. Hemingway. It's his little joke, the most sophisticated of which he is capable, and I can never bring myself to tell him it isn't funny. He is going to become something called a Petroleum Engineer, and his starting salary in two years' time will be more than I earn in a good twenty-four month period. He is twenty."

Douglas picks up his drink and stares down at the melting ice cubes intensely. Clare applauds him for his sense of the dramatic and thinks that it is Douglas, not she, who should have tried for a career on the stage.

"My older daughter is thirteen. She practices sexual tricks on me because I am a male and not someone she sees regularly. She tells me harrowing details about her life in junior high school and refuses to understand my reluctance to be a good audience. I do not want to know about the song she and her best friend have invented to celebrate the science teacher's unruly erections. I do not want to know about the Tampax Slumber Parties."

"Good grief," says Sigrid, sounding like a midwestern innocent for the first time Clare can remember. "What are they?"

"I do not want to know," repeats Douglas. "These are not appropriate subjects for a father and daughter to discuss."

"What do you want her to be like?"

"Like my youngest daughter," says Douglas. "Sally is only seven—pretty as an angel and dumb as an ox. She has her mother's nice instincts for falsity—my second wife was English, you know—and little Sally flirts like a demon and then pretends it never happened. She has a fine sense of the appropriate, my Sally."

Douglas narrows his eyes in a cynical smile and challenges Clare—or so it seems to her—to rebut this appraisal of woman's role with the same cold logic she has used on him earlier, but Clare is far too wise to fall into that trap. Instead, she chooses to laugh with the rest of them. She can just see McCloy, deep in conversation with an old harridan who appears to be leaving. Gene is bending toward the woman courteously; while she remains at the bar he will not empty her ashtray or whisk away the glass from which she has drunk. Talk about fine instincts.

"I would like to have children," says Joseph. "I think I would be a good father." His words linger in the air above them with an awkward edge. They demand to be answered.

Clare feels a great wave of admiration for Eugene pass over her. It is his humility she admires. He is the only humble man she has ever met. No. She corrects herself. Eugene is not *humble*—nasty word, implying a peasantish, self-serving lack of what Douglas might call self-esteem—but rather a man miraculously endowed with the quality of humility. There is a difference.

"I'm sure you would," says Sigrid. "I'm sure you will."

Now that the harridan has left, McCloy erases all traces of her tenure with effortless efficiency. Clare slips on her glasses, the better to appreciate his deft movements. Gene is polishing the bar with sensuous sweeps of the clean-looking rag. Clare is appalled when she focuses on that hand, that wrist, and sees it applied to her person instead of the mahogany grain.

Oh dear. In her mind's eye it is not the bar's surface but her own living flesh over which Gene's clever hands are lovingly refurbishing luster and coaxing a gleam. Humbly, with dedication, McCloy performs this duty, unaware of an audience; Clare thinks there is something unseemly about her clandestine observation of this unknown but beloved man who believes himself to be functioning privately.

"Whom would you like for the father of your child?" Douglas' tone is gentle, though mocking still. He is trying to appease her, make a joke of his own revelations. "Of course," he adds gallantly, "Joseph and I stand ready, should we be chosen. No greater honor, *et cetera.*"

Two can play at this game. "Thank you," says Clare. "It's decent of you, Douglas, but no writers need apply. I do not want my child's father to be a writer."

"Oh, I don't know," says Sigrid. "A Nobel laureate wouldn't be bad. Or even a best-seller."

"What Clare meant was no poor, unrecognized writers need apply," says Douglas.

"You miss my point," says Clare, temporarily forgetting to play and lapsing into sincerity. "It's not the financial insecurity of writers I'm worried about. It's their temperament. I'm neurotic enough by myself, on my own—why pass on two sets of neurotic genes to my innocent child?"

"I think," says Joseph, "that only psychosis—certain forms—is considered genetic."

"Personally," says Sigrid, "I would choose a blue-eyed construction worker or auto mechanic. Someone with a splendid body and a good but untutored mind."

Unfortunately, McCloy chooses this very moment to sally into the back room and retrieve the catsup bottle from the table. For the first time Clare realizes that Eugene will have to wash their glasses and tidy after them. The cook has left. Will a barman come later? She wants to ask him if she and the other hacks have been an inconvenience to him all these years, but McCloy is beaming at them as if their presence in his establishment is a continuing source of pleasure for him. When he speaks, he seems to be directing his comment mostly to Clare, but it is so unexpected she can only blink.

"It's the Ides of March," he says. "That's what the lady told me. It quite bewildered her."

"When beggars die, there are no comets seen," quotes Joseph. "The heavens themselves blaze forth the death of princes."

"Now who said that, Joe? Would it have been the old soothsayer? The one who warns Caesar early on?"

"It was his wife, actually," says Joseph glumly.

"Who else?" mutters Douglas.

"I saw the film," says Eugene. "With Marlon Brando and James Mason. It was fine." He taps the catsup bottle smartly, as if to commend it, and turns to go.

"Eugene?" Sigrid's voice recalls him. "Do you have any children?"

Clare reads in McCloy's eyes the surprise such a question is likely to generate when it comes out of nowhere. The bewilderment is terrible at first, but it swiftly tempers to a fine amalgamation of indifference and grace: the look of a man who is accustomed to answering personal questions in the line of duty.

"No," he says. "I haven't."

Clare tries to picture the child she and McCloy might produce, and finds it surprisingly easy to do so. Male or female, it would look very much like its father in the first few months. The downy hair, similar to Gene's hair now, would prefigure what was to come, and the well-turned limbs would be as neat and fresh as new, pale wood. Perhaps the child, sitting in its high chair, would feel the need to beautify its tray; it might swipe intently at the crumbs thereon because the need to make things nice was planted in the very genes.

Clare smiles, because the image of this baby is much clearer than that of the child implanted in her by Cristobal St. John.

12

Imperfect People

There is an unspoken rule among the hacks with regard to the discussion of money. Each one knows what the others are working on at any given time, what sorts of contracts they've received, the time limit imposed, perks, if any—everything but the exact amount of the advance. That information is optional, and if lies are told they are generally meant to reassure rather than to inspire envy.

Sigrid is thinking about advances throughout most of the discussion today; it is a topic much on her mind. For her latest Fiona-type book she has been offered an advance of $10,000, half on signing and half on delivery. Romances are not doing as well this year as last; it is quite possible she will earn no royalties on this book and she wonders if $10,000 is enough. She cannot ask the group to counsel her, because it will anger Douglas. She wants to get Clare alone, or even Joseph, but Douglas must not know. This is only Sigrid's seventh book, and it had taken Douglas nearly ten years to earn such an advance in pre-inflation days. It is a fact he is fond of repeating.

"A lot of these middle-aged Irish guys are bachelors," Douglas is saying now, referring to Eugene's childless state.

"I think he has a wife," says Joseph. "He mentioned her once, didn't he? Her name is Nora."

"When did he mention her?" Clare's words slur slightly now, and Sigrid envies her ability to be affected by liquor. She feels as sober now as she did upon entering the place two hours ago.

"It was when you wrote that Gothic for young adults," says Joseph. "The one without sex scenes, because they were only fifteen and virgins? I distinctly remember Gene saying, 'I think I'll take this one home to Nora.'"

"A real mental giant, Mrs. McCloy," says Douglas.

Why is it, Sigrid wonders, that the least kind person in a group is always the one whose feelings must be protected? Why must she refrain from mentioning her advance for the sake of Douglas, who never misses an opportunity to needle others? It isn't as if he had subsisted on the income of those early books alone; Douglas was in those days an editor at a high-powered magazine, only quitting after the publication of his first two Slatts detective novels convinced him he could make it as a writer. Is it her fault that the editor who had been so fond of Slatts was fired and went to work for a textbook firm?

Sigrid's entire income comes from her writing, and she can only write novels. The very idea of writing magazine articles (something the others have done frequently) sickens her. She has no desire to sign her name to a piece examining the emotional life of plants, or a self-help article designed to help women in Eau Claire or Butte or Youngstown to rid themselves of cellulite. She knows what those women are like and does not wish to solace them, but that is not the point. Sigrid treasures the anonymity and freedom she enjoys as a writer of trashy fiction. Her imagination is as fecund as the land from which she came—rich, endless, regenerative, a bottomless source.

Unlike Joey, she doesn't give a fig for any of the characters she invents, and also unlike Joey, she knows that not a single shred of herself is reborn in any of them. Sigrid's genius is for knowing what other people would imagine if they possessed her imaginative faculties; all she has to do is picture something she would dislike intensely and—presto!—she has tapped into the fantasies of her readers and knows how to proceed.

"If you try to write down," Clare once said, "they catch you. It doesn't work. That's why you have to find that little hook, that tiny snag, where you can hang something of your own. Then, just when you're sickest of your heroine and wish you could boil her in oil, you take her down from the hook and remember what made her bearable in the first place."

Sigrid can remember thinking about this comment for hours. It had the unmistakable stamp of truth, yet why, then, was the reader response to her novels so favorable? For a time she toyed with an unwholesome theory: the streak of masochism that made them cry for more rapes, more humiliations along the rocky road to true fulfillment, was broader than she had supposed. It extended to other areas of their lives, causing them to heap praise, in the questionnaires, on a woman who despised them. As is often the case, the truth was revealed to her quite casually, in the guise of an otherwise unimportant event. On the steps of her Chelsea walk-up, she encountered a pudgy young woman, perhaps two years her junior, who wanted to know if Sigrid had seen Stanley. Stanley, as it happened, lived in the apartment directly above Sigrid. He was a weedy gent, a quiet and considerate neighbor, whose chief activity seemed to be that of going to work in the morning dressed in suits whose trouser legs were always too short, and returning in the evening with a plastic carry-bag from the local Shopwell. Sigrid could not imagine why anyone should want to contact Stanley or be concerned for his whereabouts, yet the face of the woman on the stairs was desperate, ravaged.

"Are you his sister?" she asked.

"I'm his woman," said the supplicant. "I lost my key, and I've been here for two hours."

Sigrid stepped past her, murmuring reassuring words, and gained the haven of her own apartment gratefully. That evening, in front of her typewriter, she repressed frequent giggles at the thought of anyone styling herself as Stanley's "woman." That he had a woman at all seemed so comical the very thought distracted her from her writing, and presently she went to sit at her window to watch the street life below. Almost immediately, as if by design, a taxi slid to a halt in front of the building and Stanley emerged from the passenger's door. He was not carrying his usual bag and advanced to the front door with a determined gait. She heard his steps on the landing, and then a great female cry of relief as he was sighted on the stairs. Footfalls thundered, voices mingled, and Sigrid was drawn to the peephole in her door to make some sense of what had happened.

She was never to know the source of the small drama, but what she did see explained her success as a novelist once and for all. Framed in the eye of the peephole, Stanley and his lover embraced with all the fervor of Sigrid's pulp creations; she could see Stanley's hands buried deep in the black haystack of the girl's hair, see the transfiguring expression of ecstasy on her face, the eyes squeezed shut, tears making their way down her pear-shaped face as she arched her neck to burrow against him and murmur fervid words against his polyester lapel. She could even see the trembling of Stanley's fingers as he splayed them on her back in approved bodice-ripper style, and the answering thrust of her bunchy, unfortunately shaped body.

Long after they ascended the stairs, Sigrid remained at the peephole, marveling that the coming together of these two ugly and insignificant people should so transport her. When she realized, gradually and then with perfect conviction, that she envied them, she smiled with ferocious delight. A problem had been solved, and she could go to bed in a state of blessed purity. Envy for those less perfect than herself was the secret of her success. Imperfect people wished to read about their experiences, but because it would not do to draw heroes with comical trouser legs and heroines with flabby arms, they wished to see themselves disguised. She had always known that the elemental passions she wrote about were the province of people she would never choose to speak to, but never before had she been presented with such a graphic illustration.

She went to sleep that night reconciled to her envy. It had no more place in her life, as she saw it, than the passing jealousy a human being might feel for the antics of a caged monkey, so endearingly free, as it picks at itself for all the world to see.

Clare and Joseph are conferring about something, heads close together, while Douglas stares off into the bleak afternoon beyond the windows. In repose, his face is sad and kind. Sigrid feels great affection for this man, even though he is the sole member of the group who knows she is a compulsive liar and frequently telegraphs this knowledge her way; she loves Douglas for being such a mess, and respects him because he has, as they say, her number. She touches his arm, and he flinches.

"Twenty-one books and three children," says Sigrid. "Not bad."

Douglas' mustache twitches violently. Sigrid can actually see the process by which he converts emotion to venom break down. He wants terribly to answer her in his usual flippant style, but the whiskey and whatever it is that has made him so edgy today have combined to break his circuits. Douglas gives her an incredulous look and smiles sheepishly.

Sigrid suddenly yearns to make them all happy, these people whom she loves. She loves them because they are her adopted family. Like a real family, they do not claim much of her attention and only have to be seen twice a month, but unlike a real family they are brave and clever, despite their faults, and able to surprise her occasionally. By virtue of her age, she ought to be the daughter, with Clare and Douglas as parents and Joey as a slightly older brother, but generally she feels she is the mother. It doesn't matter, in any case. Mother or daughter or sister, she longs to comfort them. She is very democratic in this way; if she had possessed the apparatus for comforting the woman on the stairs she would have done so, but she does not know how.

Vaguely, she feels that a sexual overture in Douglas' direction would be in order, but she has no talent in these matters. Joseph would surely profit from some wise and motherly gesture on her part, but they are too close in age and he would misinterpret it. And what of Clare, whom she loves too? She could tell Clare that she herself has long since had a child and the event was of little importance to her, but that is not what Clare wishes to hear. Sigrid knows she is badly equipped for giving comfort, and soothes herself with a wondrous fantasy.

If she could, Sigrid would write happy endings for all of them. She wishes they were blank sheets of paper she could roll into her typewriter, there to be made joyous and triumphant, after many pages of travail.

13

A Queens Father

At a little past four, the time when the hacks generally leave, they seem to have settled in for the afternoon. McCloy is made uneasy by their continued presence and remembers, guiltily, his earlier image of Clare trapped at the bar on St. Patrick's night. Outside the light is failing fast, and the last of his cloth caps has gone. These hours are the doldrums of Eugene's day. From now until six, when his backup barman arrives for the evening trade, very little happens.

McCloy takes the newspaper Maxine has left behind and scans the headlines, sitting on the perch where he had leafed through *Fiona's Folly*. He opens the paper and sees an article about nuclear submarines, a picture of Ronald Reagan. McCloy slips on his reading glasses and confronts the President. Something shifty there. It's in the eyes. Facing him is a story about a Queens father who has broken every rib in his son's body because the lad will not stop wetting the bed. The child is eighteen months of age. On previous occasions, it seems, lighted cigarettes have been applied to the soles of his feet. McCloy removes his glasses and looks out the window again.

Although, as the owner of a bar, he is the legal possessor of a .38, he has never had occasion to use it. He has had to break up some fights in his time, and because he does not enjoy violence, he is very efficient at stopping it, despite his smallish size. Now it occurs to him that it would give him great pleasure to seek out the Queens father, carrying the gun he has never fired except on a practice range when he was first licensed, and put a bullet through his head. Nothing sadistic, no pain—because, of course, that would place him on a level with the man he came to punish—but a clean, efficient removal of what should not be permitted to live.

Sigrid's question had nearly knocked him on his heels for a moment there. At first he had been angry—what possible reason could she have to ask him such a thing?—but then he had realized it was a friendly sort of question. He had replied in a friendly fashion, by telling only half the truth, or rather by leaving things unsaid, because to put them fully in the picture would surely have caused them all great discomfort.

McCloy's son Tim has been dead for ten years now. He would have been fifteen this October, and probably quite tall, for McCloy's wife was a tall woman and the boy had favored her. Tim had walked early, lurching to his feet of a sudden when he was nine months old and astounding his mother by staggering across the room with demented determination. "Of course," the stern pediatrician had told them, "physical coordination has nothing to do with intelligence." Yet it seemed to Eugene that his son was abundantly gifted in realms other than the physical. Tim also talked early, using the kind of verbal shorthand appropriate to a baby who has not had time yet to learn the niceties of grammar. At one, for example, he was fond of saying "Want bananas!" Several months later he had refined the message to "Bananas for Tim now." Bananas, sliced and swimming in milk, were the child's favorite food, and even today Eugene turns away when he sees pyramids of bananas gaily stacked in the Korean fruit stalls along Broadway.

At the age of two, Tim had driven his mother to distraction by the sheer volume of questions he was able to ask. They were not the sort of children's questions once popularized in a show called "Kids Say the Darnedest Things." Tim would ask why nothing good to eat was colored blue; why his Aunt Nora laughed when nothing was funny; if carpets and armchairs died, like goldfish, and got flushed down the toilet. Always, Eugene endeavored to answer his son's questions in the same earnest spirit in which they were asked, but Tim's appetite for knowledge so far exceeded his ability to comprehend that father and son were equally frustrated. They emerged from these sessions of intellectual bantering, the grown man and the little boy—scarcely more than a baby—weary but fond and forgiving. McCloy can remember aching for his son to be a few years older, so they could talk properly. He can also remember how his wife, Pat, was forever cautioning him to bear in mind that Tim was only a baby. Mother and son had an easy, rolling relationship in which they battled and made up, battled and made up again, like lovers in one of the books Clare or Sigrid wrote. He sees them now, Pat towering in her long-legged, raggedy-haired glory over the repentant child, waiting for him to succumb to her superior power and charm, enfolding him in her arms when he sidled his way to her and admitted that her resources were greater than his, and smiling over Tim's shoulder as if to say: *You see? This is between us. My son and me. You can't possibly understand, Gene. Flesh of my flesh. Ripped from my body, not yours.*

He never resented her for these potent, mute demonstrations of her greater claim on the boy—Pat had indeed had such a terrible time bringing him to life that the doctors said she could never have another—but watched them both with a vigilance born of love and fearfulness. McCloy was then, and is now, naturally fearful. He expects the worst, and time has proved him right.

"Are you a gambling man, Gene?"

It is Joseph, standing directly in front of him. McCloy has not even noticed and wonders how long Joey has been waiting.

"There was a time," McCloy says, "when I was keen on the horses. Not so much any more. I enjoy a good poker game now and then."

Joseph looks disappointed. "Why did you quit the horses?" he asks.

"Dropped too much money, Joe. It's a tricky business." McCloy understands, at last, how Joseph has acquired the expensive cowboy boots and the Walkman. No doubt he is still enveloped in the rosy cloud of beginner's luck and thinks he has tapped a whole new source of income. It is precisely this naïveté of Joseph's that makes McCloy apprehensive; he wishes he could guide and help Joseph but thinks it is not his province. Nevertheless, he makes a stab. Lowering his voice and leaning forward confidentially, he says,

"Don't go thinking, just because you've made a few lucky picks, that the track will be good to you, Joe. And don't bet on an unknown because you like the name. And above all, don't ever do business with a bookie who wants to give you credit, because then you'll be into the shylocks." He realizes, as soon as he has uttered the word "shylock," that the lad might think him an anti-Semite. "Loan sharks," he amends.

But Joseph is looking merely bewildered, not offended. "I just went to the OTB a few times," he says. "I'm not a heavy-duty gambler, Gene. I've never won more than thirty dollars, actually." He indicates politely his desire for another beer, his movements much slower now than when he arrived, his reflexes less sure. "I asked about the gambling," he explains, "because one of the characters in my latest book plays the horses a lot. Eventually, he's going to get in deep trouble."

"One of Hawk's friends?" Gene likes to show Joey he remembers.

"It's a different book," Joseph says evasively. "A novel about a compulsive gambler." Now his voice is the one that is lowered. He glances over his shoulder as if to make sure he is not overheard. "I haven't even mentioned it to the group yet." He drinks straight from the bottle McCloy has placed before him. "This man," he murmurs, "loses everything—his wife—everything—because of the gambling."

"Certainly I've known men like him. My sister Nora was married to a gambler." Joseph is staring so morosely down into the neck of the bottle that Gene thinks he hasn't heard him, but presently he stirs himself and blinks.

"I won't say any more about this book, Gene. Not for now. But maybe next time we meet I'll be needing your, uh, insights. I'd appreciate it, you know, just between the two of us."

"Any time," says McCloy.

Joseph gives him a little salute and lurches back to the table, but before he reaches his destination he halts, backtracks, and returns to the bar. "Nora," he says, "is your sister?" He waits for the affirming nod, then smiles craftily and leaves.

McCloy is saved from further introspection by the ringing of the phone. It is his barman, informing McCloy that he will be half an hour late tonight on account of a postponed dental appointment. No sooner has the phone been replaced in its cradle than it rings again; this time it is Nora, almost as if the mention of her name has prompted her to call, who wants to know if he will be home for dinner.

"No," he says, "I told you, Nora. Tonight I'll be staying on."

"You didn't tell me," she says. "You never said a word." Her voice has the hectoring note of a stock wife. Anyone hearing her would picture her in those terms, see her as a stout woman in a chenille bathrobe, curlers in her hair, rolling pin at the ready, the very image of the comical character—what was her name?—in the cartoon strip McCloy had liked so much several decades ago. And yet Nora is quite the reverse of this image. She is dainty and thin, with marvelous hair and the noble wreck of once-beautiful bones apparent in her face.

For years, Nora has known that Tuesday is one of Gene's late nights. It is a fact as immutable as church on Sunday and bingo on Friday, but still she calls and assures him, each Tuesday, of his selfishness in not giving her notice. McCloy knows his older sister so well he can assess, within a drink, how deeply she has dented the gin and cranberry juice so far today. Her voice, bullying and slightly slurred, tells him she has been moderate. On truly hectic days, Nora speaks with the haughty precision of a schoolmistress who knows her pupils snicker behind her back.

McCloy apologizes for his lack of consideration and tells her not to wait up for him. Because he has been thinking about Tim, he wants to say something affectionate and soothing to this last surviving member of his family, but try as he will, he cannot come up with anything not fraught with potential horror.

"Alright then, girl?" he says.

"No consideration," says Nora, and hangs up.

McCloy, holding the humming receiver in his hand, sees his sister as she must be, this moment, in the house they now share in Queens. It is identical to the house he once inhabited with his wife and son, is, in fact, only four doors away from the house of his marriage. Nora will be standing at the kitchen wall phone, in precisely the same architectural location where Pat was wont to conduct her telephone conversations. Whereas Pat used to lean against the wall and motion for cigarettes (the cord was never long enough to permit her to retrieve her pack from the kitchen table), Nora will stand well away from the apparatus and replace the phone in its cradle with exaggerated respect. It is the difference, McCloy thinks, between being born here or over there. Nora has never become thoroughly American.

Voices live there! Tim, quite young—when was he not?—once pointed to the kitchen telephone and whispered these words to his father, and how Gene laughed!

McCloy walks around the bar, barely knowing what his mission is, and approaches the back room. His earlier desire to kill the monstrous man he has read about in the paper is utterly gone; if some all-powerful chronicler were to remind him of his murderous instincts he would call him a liar. All Eugene seeks now is distraction. He approaches Joseph as he might a doctor or a pusher of drugs.

"Joe," he asks humbly, interrupting the conversation without his customary apology, "do you think I might borrow the little machine for a bit? As long as you're not using it, I mean."

Joseph looks up in confusion.

"The music machine."

"Your Walkman, Joey," says Clare.

"Well, sure," says Joseph, beaming hugely. He takes the machine from his pocket, fumbling a little, and hands it over to McCloy with a flourish.

"A convert!" says Joseph. "Be my guest."

14

The WLA

Douglas is feeling quite drunk now, and he doesn't mind a bit. His earlier chagrin at the lower toleration for alcohol the years have brought him has vanished, and in its stead comes a sly, complacent conviction: everything is just fine, absolutely as it should be. He will go home, drink black coffee, and polish off the penultimate chapter of the Irish saga novel, killing Eileen Hennessy as they have planned in committee. Then he will treat himself to a late dinner at the Mexican restaurant on Bleecker he likes, make the rounds of a few bars, and hit the sack. Tomorrow, when the woman he has been seeing returns from a business trip to Philadelphia, he will tell her about the thing which so upset him today. He will make it into a poignant but amusing story, preferably before they go to bed, and she will not know whether to laugh with him or stamp her narrow, patrician foot in outrage. Her fine ambivalence is something Douglas counts on heavily; the most desirable characteristic a woman can manifest for him is uncertainty.

"Let's have one more drink," he says. "On the Ides of March a person ought to get pissed as a newt."

"I would have thought the opposite," says Sigrid. "A person should remain alert and suspicious on the Ides of March."

Clare laughs and offers no reason for her merriment. It is Joseph who chooses to become pedantic and fatuous. "You said *remain,*" Joseph challenges. "As if being alert and suspicious were a natural state, Sig."

"It is, for her," says Douglas. "Sigrid would make a fabulous terrorist. Can't you see her in the Baader-Meinhof Gang?"

"How ridiculous," says Clare. "Please, Douglas." She is still laughing, and Douglas realizes that his image of Sigrid as terrorist has neatly tapped into one of her own private views—Clare laughs because she has had the same idea more than once. Her helpless laughter elates him; he embroiders on the fantasy to prolong it.

"Sigrid has the potential to become the first terrorist spokesman for writers," he says. "Those fingers might have been designed for the wiring of delicate bombs. I see her scurrying down the corridors of Doubleday searching for a broom closet, tapping out communiqués to be read by the press, kidnapping major editors at gunpoint and holding them hostage in the Chelsea Hotel."

"What will my demands be?" Sigrid asks.

Douglas holds up one hand, ticks off his points. "For the release of"—he mentions a much-hated editor—"the Writers' Liberation Army demands *immediate* payment of all advance and royalty monies owed to writers everywhere and now accruing interest for the publishers. We also demand the abolition of the Best Seller list, detention and deportation of all publishing personnel who buy books using computers to determine the commercial success of said books, and the assurance of *The New York Times* that worthy paperback originals will be reviewed. These terms are not negotiable. *Freedom and Respect for all our comrades slaving in the dungeons of hackdom!*"

"What an idea," says Joseph. "It's an idea whose time has come. You left out some demands, though. I want some say in my covers, for example."

"That's going too far," says Douglas.

"You—of all people! Don't you remember when the artist made

your heroine's hair black when it was supposed to be red? You said you had to go through the whole book and change 'flaming' to 'raven' and it ruined the scene with the Indians." Clare is quite indignant. "There were all these Indians staring in awe at hair that was exactly like their own."

"True," says Douglas. "We'll demand some cover supervision."

"Longer legs for Laird Bruce," says Joseph, "and a face for my Hawk that doesn't make him look like a gay waiter."

"I want the expression 'track record' stricken from the language of publishers," says Clare. "I see red when people talk about a writer's track record. That's my demand."

"All right," says Douglas. "That's six points. The Writers' Liberation Army is not a greedy organization. We do not require expensive aircraft or ask any money except what is due us."

"Wait a minute," says Sigrid. "I thought *I* was the terrorist, Douglas. You say I'd make a good terrorist and then you take over."

"You are back at the Chelsea Hotel holding that son of a bitch hostage, Sig. You do all the operations that require skill and daring and cruelty, while Clare and Joe and I think things out."

"What if our demands aren't met? Do I have to shoot him?" Sigrid is smiling unpleasantly.

"That is your prerogative, of course, but I would prefer to go about it differently. I would sentence him to read, over and over again, all the shitty books he's paid so many millions to acquire. It would be a life sentence, worse than death."

"I wouldn't shoot him under any circumstances," says Sigrid. "Contrary to what you might think, I am not in the least cruel. It would disgust me to hurt anyone."

"Of course," says Douglas in falsely soothing tones, "of course you're not cruel that way, Sigrid. But who could know it, looking at you? You're scary-looking."

This pronouncement makes everyone uneasy, Douglas thinks, because it is true. Sigrid is scary because she is so lacking in any external flaws. She is far less beautiful than Clare, but unlike Clare she is never rumpled, blemished, touched by weariness or illness, dressed inappropriately, rearranged by wind or rain. He has never seen her with dirty hair or chapped lips, never detected a thread of red in the clear whites of her eyes, never spied a run-down heel or button about to come loose. He cannot imagine her naked, and sometimes suspects that beneath her clothes there is no real body—only two seamlessly joined plastic moldings simulating the form of a woman.

"Douglas is afraid of your Protestant eyes," says Joseph, trying to lighten things up. "Even though he's a WASP too, he fears the power of blue eyes that have looked out on prairies. He was born in New York, remember."

"Too silly," says Clare. "You're all quite drunk, except for Sig. Stop picking on her."

"Okay," says Douglas, tired of trying to provoke the unflappable Sigrid into some semblance of sexual combat. "But if we ever form the Writers' Liberation Army, I say she should be our spokesperson."

While the others think up additional demands—Joseph has actually produced a pen and is jotting words down on the back of a Harp coaster—Douglas rehearses his planned confession for tomorrow. The upsetting incident seems so much less worthy of his anxiety, now that he has numerous whiskeys beneath his belt, that he begins to wonder if it is worth relating, after all. He had planned to begin with a description of the branch library near Eugene's, quickly sketch it in for her: the rows of scarred tables, littered with copies of old newspapers, at which sat eccentrically dressed old people who had nowhere to go during the long afternoon; the surly, illiterate women who checked the books out so reluctantly it was clear that any form of work was beneath their dignity; the dog-eared paperback romances, donated, not acquired, that seemed to be the library's most sought-after form of literature; the discarded crust of someone's lunchtime sandwich tucked away in the card cataloge—Douglas reckons his corporate lady love will be both amused and depressed by his description of the moribund little library.

"But, Douglas," she will say, analytical always, "why do you ever set foot in such a place?"

Douglas will explain that he arrived early for the Tuesday lunch and, having some small point of research to check for his Irish novel, popped in for a quick look at the Britannica. This will have the advantage of being partially truthful, since his first visit to the branch library over a year ago was made in just such circumstances.

"How's this?" Joseph holds one of the Harp coasters up for approval. On the back he has sketched a crude drawing of a clenched, revolutionary fist raised in defiance. The fist is clutching an enormous pen, and from the pen's nib flow the words FREEDOM NOW! "It's the logo for the WLA," Joseph says. "At first I thought of a man chained to his typewriter, but that didn't seem to have a rebellious feel to it. We could do those as leaflets."

Douglas wonders, briefly, if Joey has gone around the bend, but the three of them are so delighted with themselves—even Sigrid—that he is reassured. The idea of the Writers' Liberation Army has provided them with enough amusement to see them through the rest of the afternoon.

"I want another drink," says Douglas. "I thought we were going to have one more round."

"Oh, but look at Gene," says Clare. "What a shame it would be to disturb him."

Douglas sees that McCloy is lost to the world. Wearing Joseph's Walkman, he is leaning at the far end of the bar, looking out at Broadway. He can see only a thin crescent of McCloy's profile, but what he sees seems so tranquil and beatified he understands Clare's reluctance to disturb the man. On the other hand, her maternal tones, her obstinate insistence (whether she knows it or not) on romanticizing a perfectly ordinary working-class Irish bar owner so annoy him he wants to trip her out of her chair.

"What a shame it would be to disturb him," he says, imitating her soppy voice. "What's he here for, Clare? To find salvation in a Sony Walkman?"

"Am I going to have to pour you into a cab?" asks Clare disdainfully.

"You've had quite a lot of Scotch," says Sigrid, smiling her superior smile.

Bitches! At least his corporate woman is in awe of him because he is a writer, just as he is in awe of her competence—she, who flies first-class in the service of her corporation and transacts complex business, at once dull and magical, in cities he has no desire to visit. That's the way it should be between men and women, thinks Douglas. Awe and contempt, mystery and boredom—these are the ingredients necessary for any interaction between the sexes. He will never be able to function properly in the presence of Clare and Sigrid, because he is not a mystery to them. They are like a group of jocks, whiling away a bleak afternoon, all too aware of one another's special gifts, and not inclined to be impressed by them. He looks to Joey for support, but Joey is busy sketching another logo for the WLA.

Douglas gets to his feet and walks heavily toward the bar. He slips under the hatch near the cash register and begins to assemble another round of drinks. It takes quite a long time, because he is not sure where to find the Tabasco for the girls' Bloody Marys. He pours Sigrid an especially stiff drink—*let's see her lose that corncob-up-the-ass attitude,* he thinks—and makes a notation of the new round on a cocktail napkin so Gene will know he doesn't mean to cheat him. McCloy must have the volume turned up high, for Douglas can hear a faraway, tinny sound of strings, even at this distance.

When it comes time to make his own drink, Douglas pauses, and then splashes twice the usual amount into his glass. Carefully, he marks the number 2 on the napkin, to signify that he has had a double. He gathers the drinks in his large hands and prepares to return to the table. He is not even sure whether he has enough cash to pay for this afternoon's food and drink, but he knows his credit is good.

At the end of the bar, McCloy is motionless. He had not even noticed the poacher on his preserve.

At the table, the others have begun a chant. Joseph leads it, raising his hand with clenched fist. *What do we want?* he cries.

Freedom!

When do we want it?

Now!

15

Hawks and Doves

Joseph has never been much of a drinker and now, having consumed so many beers in a mere few hours, he is roaring drunk. Hawk can drink all night, tossing back shots of his favorite beverage, Jack Daniels, without ever slurring a word or stumbling; because Joseph is so temperate, he overestimated the amount a real drinker could salt away in a night and had to be reprimanded by an editor on completion of his first desert warfare book. "He's a *lush,*" the old editor, himself a veteran of World War II, had said. "Christ, Joe, this man has to drive a goddamn tank through the desert under *harrowing* conditions! The alcohol content in his blood is just about approaching the lethal level here."

Embarrassed, Joseph had reduced the number of drinks Hawk consumed at officers' clubs and exotic bars by more than two-thirds. Even so, drinking straight Jack Daniels, Hawk could still put Joseph under the table any day. Joseph feels, as the clock above the bar approaches five, that he has acquired some Hawkish attributes over the long afternoon. He does not understand why and is too elated to ponder the reasons for this exalted feeling. He does not know that he is shouting, or that his design for the Writers' Liberation Army would appear to him, when sober, as a scrawl that might have been executed by a child. He only knows that he feels heroic, invincible, well loved, and witty. He remembers the Joseph who was blubbering in the men's room because of some sentimental reflex as a character he might have written months ago. Of no importance at this time. He swaggers off to the same place now, bladder bursting, and laughs aloud when he sees the HARNESS SORROW graffito. His urine is released in a powerful, bullish stream. Of course, in the desert warfare series, one never mentions processes of excretion, but this is, he knows, exactly the way Hawk pisses.

"WLA!" he cries, returning to the table.

"All the way!" shouts Clare fondly.

"How did you know what to say?" says Sigrid. "How do you know the right responses?"

"Haven't you ever been in a demonstration?" Clare lights her cigarette at the wrong end and wrinkles her nose as an acrid smell hovers over the table. She crushes the cigarette out and pushes the pack away. "You sort of learn the responses at political demonstrations," she says. "You can second-guess the chants."

"How interesting," says Sigrid. "It's the sort of thing I wouldn't know about."

"Civil disobedience is not Sig's thing," says Douglas.

"I suppose," says Sigrid, "you all marched against the war in Vietnam?"

"While you were husking corn, or getting your first period," says Douglas, "you imagine us all on the barricades?"

"I'm only asking, Douglas. There's no need to be excessively insulting."

"I've never marched for anything," says Douglas. "The sight of my second wife striding along under a feminist banner was quite enough for me. It must have been her English blood—she thought she was Emmeline Pankhurst or something. Shoulder to shoulder."

Joseph and Clare compare notes and discover that they have been in many of the same places long before they met. They have participated in the great anti–Vietnam War march in Washington, although neither was tear-gassed; between them, they have protested against nuclear armament, poverty in the ghettos, apartheid in South Africa, American intervention in Latin America, British rule in the North of Ireland, budget cuts, book-banning, police brutality, pesticides, the oppression of women and of homosexuals of both sexes. Clare has even engaged in these activities on foreign soil—in London, she marched with a cadre of women dedicated to eradicating wife abuse.

"I wish the topic had never been introduced," says Douglas. "I didn't know you two were professional agitators."

"I think it's sweet," says Sigrid. "Imagine caring."

"Come on," says Douglas. "People go to those things to get laid. It's like a huge singles' bar with righteous overtones."

Joseph bounds forward with his new Hawkish authority. "Not true," he says aggressively. "Nothing could have been further from my mind or more removed from my expectations." He does not hear his voice pronouncing the word as *extapations.* He earnestly wishes to explain himself to Douglas, but even in his muddled state he knows the explanation will invite ridicule. Aside from the Vietnam demonstrations, which he took part in when he was still in high school, his experiences in civil disobedience have all been choreographed, orchestrated, by Vivvy. It was she who was keen on Save the Earth demos, she who made him feel that a refusal to march for Women's Rights was tantamount to spitting on the marriage contract.

Clare leaps in to save him, temporarily, from justifying his actions to Douglas. "Cynicism is all very well in its way, Douglas, but you take it too far. Too far. To be as doubtful of the motives of others as you are is just as naive as to trust them all the time. I, personally, have seldom seen anyone on a picket line who has roused me sexually. One goes because one has convictions, no matter how rarely one has a chance to express them in one's line of work."

"So," says Douglas, with a particularly nasty smile, "if one writes rape fantasies one feels obliged to march for Women's Lib?"

"It's not a matter of guilt, is it, Joey? Guilt has nothing to do with it. No. Definitely not. Not for us. Writers lead uniquely solitary lives, as I'm sure you'd all agree. We are, ourselves, oppressed—more sinned against than sinning. Surely guilt need not play a part in our quest for social justice."

Drunkenly, pedantically, Clare warms to her topic. Joseph is intrigued by this facet of Clare's personality, which he has never before seen; admiration for her fierce demeanor mixes with gratitude (she has taken the spotlight away from him), and he wants very much to see how she will divorce herself from guilt. Although he will not admit it, guilt loomed so large in his life during his marriage to Vivvy that he can hardly imagine voicing the sentiments emerging so effortlessly from his fellow hack. What placed him in those sweaty, loud, endless events they are discussing, if not guilt?

"I believe three types of human beings participate in demonstrations," says Clare. "The first are, of course, those directly involved, those with a stake in the outcome. The second are the wretched guilty, who think they can atone for their uneasiness at leading tolerably comfortable lives, while most of the world writhes about in utter misery, by shouting slogans and placing themselves at risk. Usually minimal risk. The third, to which Joey and I belong, are creatures with an imaginative faculty so grotesquely overdeveloped we can picture exactly what it would be like to be truly *unfortunate*. We actually feel the cattle-prod, the bullet, the napalm, the hunger, the fist in the kidneys, the powerlessness, the despair—" Clare has run out of things to feel for the moment and turns to Joseph with passionate need for confirmation. "Don't we, Joe? Isn't that how it is with you?"

"Sure!" says Joseph, who has never in his life made the appalling transformation from horrid fact to intimate feeling Clare boasts of. "It's our grotesquely overdeveloped imaginations!"

"Under the circumstances," says Clare, "it's the least one can do."

"What I want to know," says Sigrid, "is why isn't it more sexy? You said no one roused you on the barricades, yet you make it sound quite exciting in a perverse sort of way."

Joseph and Clare trade glances; they alone know the secret. Joseph wonders if Clare will be truly honest, and then it occurs to him that perhaps it is his secret only—a male secret, rooted in the very guilt or insecurity Clare pretends to deny.

"That's easy," says Clare, lighting her cigarette at the correct end this time. "One always feels foolish. You can't feel sexy if you suspect you're a fool. You don't see the others, only yourself—right, Joey?" She inhales deeply. "I mean, if you're like us?"

Joseph exhales with relief. "Right," he says staunchly. "I almost always felt like an asshole."

"Chanting those responses, like in church!"

"I wouldn't know about church, but all that yelling—more like football games in high school." Joseph suddenly remembers how very much he disliked going to demonstrations with Vivvy. "Carrying those posters—you never knew which slogan you'd get—and sometimes those cumbersome banners that bellied out and hit the person in front of you."

"The linking of arms. *Too* artificial and embarrassing."

"The cops who looked like your uncle. Mine, anyway."

"The speeches. The terrible prose. Singing "We Shall Overcome." In the wrong key. For me."

"Trying not to wince when you passed the sound truck. Fearing permanent impairment to the ears."

"Still, the linking of arms was the worst."

"Talk about misanthropy," says Douglas gleefully. "You two make me seem like a saint. What frauds you are!"

"You're missing the point," says Sigrid. "Clare and Joseph were all the more heroic for attending events which embarrassed them. I think it's admirable."

Clare nods. "Thank you, Sig. It isn't that I didn't *want* to feel moved. Certainly I did, and sometimes—very occasionally—I was, but of what importance was my emotional state? Nil. Warm bodies and strong lungs are needed at political demonstrations, not egos."

"Question," says Douglas, raising his arm like a schoolboy. "Are we more heroic, as writers, because we write things that embarrass us?" He is addressing the question to Joseph.

Joseph has been amusing himself by imagining Hawk at a Gay Rights rally, but the image isn't as funny as he'd hoped. His euphoria is fading rapidly. He feels he is a man of little character, a man who can be bullied into doing things he does not wish to do. This would never happen to Douglas or Sigrid; as for Clare, at least she is her own bully. Clare, too, has character. Joseph feels he is a kind person, one who would confer social equality and justice on everyone if it were in his power, but he has never been intensely moved by anything not directly related to himself.

Douglas repeats the question. Merciless, he is.

"What is this," says Joseph, "'Youth Wants to Know?'"

"I've hit a sore spot," says Douglas. "Ole Douglas can read the minds of fellow writers. He knows your secret, Joey."

Joseph looks into Douglas' eyes and sees, deep behind the surface—the drunken man's over-earnest stare—what he has feared. Douglas does know his secret. He cannot possibly know the details—the Vivaldi that helps Joseph harness his sorrow, the decision, which he now sees as cowardly, to make his own character a compulsive gambler instead of a second-rate writer—but he has guessed the important thing. He knows Joseph is furtively writing a real novel.

"How irritating you are, Douglas," says Clare. "What is Joey's secret?"

Joseph waits to see if the melancholy in Douglas' gaze will triumph over the malice. Douglas can choose, now, to lambast him as a presumptuous hypocrite, a secret luster after fame in the Real World, a defector. He can censure him.

A very long minute passes, during which the muscle in Douglas' cheek remains mysteriously calm, and then he shrugs and indicates that it was just a tipsy joke. He has opted for peace after all.

Joseph is grateful, but damage has been done. Already, the secret pages of his manuscript, so carefully kept away from his other writings, seem less important.

Douglas scribbles something on his Harp coaster and passes it to him when Clare excuses herself to go to the ladies' room and Sigrid's attention is diverted. Joseph looks down and sees, written in Douglas' curiously neat hand, *Et tu, Brute?*

16

A Mortal Woman

On the walls of the ladies' room there are no clever, obscene, or literary phrases scrawled, only the occasional couplings of names. In Clare's stall there are three such valentines: *Mick & Mary, Johnny & Sheila,* and a new one, *Angelo & Bernie.*

Angelo and Bernie disturb Clare because she cannot imagine how either of them gained entrance to the ladies' room. Then it occurs to her that Bernie is, of course, Bernadette, and a fit of giggles seizes her. When it passes, she tries to picture this new couple. She has long since imagined what Mick & Mary and all the others are like, but Angelo & Bernie are a different matter. Bernadette has chosen an Italian lover rather than an Irish one. Do her parents mind? Or is Bernadette old enough to call her own shots? Does Angelo drink at Eugene's, or does he merely allow Bernadette to stop in now and then for a round with her cronies? Now that Bernadette has found true love, perhaps she will not drink in bars again. This may be her farewell note.

It touches Clare that the women always write the man's name first at Eugene's. Even in this totally female preserve, where no man can judge them, they confer on their lovers the honor of always going first.

Clare washes her hands, notices in the mirror that her dark, unruly hair is standing up in unbecoming tufts and whorls. In fact, bending closer and squinting for better vision, she sees the reflection of a drunken woman. Her features look somehow smeared, her color is high. This will never do. Clare pulls a comb from her bag and drags it through her hair perfunctorily, and then, because she really does not want to look like a slattern, with real energy. When she has worked for a bit, her hair, as far as she can see it, is restored to its natural state. It is thick, curly, and lustrous, and of a shade nearly black, only beginning to sport the odd grey strand. No matter how hard Clare works on it, it will never be a mass of flowing, blue-black silk (or a river of honey, a mane of fire), because Clare is a mortal woman rather than the heroine of a bodice-ripper.

She replaces the comb in her bag and turns on the cold-water tap, making a little basin of her hands and lowering her head to dash the water on her feverish face. She pats her skin dry with a paper towel, wondering if Mary, Sheila, or Bernadette have ever performed these ablutions in Gene's ladies' room, and examines the results. Yes, better. The face in the mirror is quite acceptable now; beneath its canopy of now orderly hair it is the face of an exceedingly pretty, perhaps beautiful, mortal woman who happens to be thirty-eight years old.

Clare searches for the particular eyeliner pencil she likes. She has been faithful to this brand of pencil for twenty years, even though it is increasingly hard to find these days, because with it she can perform a trick that transforms her dark eyes from the "beautiful, beautiful brown eyes" of the old song her father used to sing to her to something resembling the "huge, dark pools of liquid velvet" she has given to some of her heroines.

The pencil is not to be found in the chaos of Clare's handbag. Patiently, she sifts again and again through the objects encountered there without success. At last she sits cross-legged on the cool tile floor and methodically removes the contents of the bag. She places her wallet and comb, her keys and the police whistle her building's security patrol has given each tenant, before her; she extracts a tube of sugarless mints, a letter from a friend who lives in Paris, a felt-tipped marker, a receipt for her laundry, a bill from her allergist, a ChapStick, a purse-size atomizer of L'Air du Temps, and a handbill for a spiritualist thrust at her on the street. Nothing remains but a fine rubble of tobacco seeds and small bits of paper. She has left the pencil at home.

Clare sits on the floor regarding the contents of her bag. It does not seem essential to return to the table immediately—she has plenty of time to rest here, gathering strength and replenishing her considerable energies. No one will miss her; they are all far too drunk. She closes her eyes and instantly sees Cristobal St. John. He is riding toward her on a horse, a black Spanish stallion?—no, that's a galleon—a black Arabian stallion. The horse's coat matches Cristobal's hair, which blows back from his dark face, and even at this distance Cristobal's cornflower eyes, so shocking beneath the brooding black brows, can be seen to be flashing like blue hellfire. He is laughing, easy and proud in his young manhood, his thighs effortlessly gripping the flanks of the savage animal no one else has been able to tame.

Closer he gallops, and closer, until Clare can see the expression of eagerness and longing in those astounding blue eyes—Cristobal is urging his steed on at such a pace to hasten to the side of the woman he loves. He does not notice Clare, of course, because she is invisible, creating him, but looks beyond her to the place where a creature of unimaginable beauty waits beneath a chestnut tree, her fiery banner of hair rippling in the breeze. Her name is Philomena; she is nineteen years old.

He dismounts in one smooth, muscular movement, literally throwing himself from the horse, and in three strides he is at his lady's side. He pulls her violently into his arms, looks down into her exquisite face and murmurs inarticulate words of helpless passion, and then kisses her rose-petal lips as if he were dying of thirst and Philomena's mouth alone could save his life.

Clare opens her eyes and begins to replace the objects scattered on the floor in her bag. The scene plays itself out whether her eyes are open or closed; she sees, not the police whistle and comb in her hand, but the way in which Cristobal and Philomena will slowly sink to the grassy meadow floor. Unlike real people, they are able to go from a standing to a prone position, still wrapped in each other's arms, without injury. There are no awkward moments, no ants or sharp twigs in the grass, no impediments to their passion as they scale the peaks of ecstasy.

Clare is democratic in her fantasizing—in the book she is writing she obeys the conventions of the genre and pays attention to Philomena's sexual sensations only; now, hunkering on the tiles and restocking her purse, she gives equal time to Cristobal. She knows exactly the sort of sound he makes during orgasm—a sweet, sighing moan; she also knows that his eyes squeeze shut so tightly the tips of his long black eyelashes alone are visible. Several muscles in his back quiver endearingly. When she returns to the writing of the actual book, she must be careful to erase all traces of his vulnerability during the sexual act. Bodice-ripper heroes are strong, silent, and fierce. They do, and are not done to.

Clare gets to her feet and brushes off the back of her skirt. It angers her sometimes, having to portray her darling Cristobal in such one-dimensional terms when he is so much more. He, the real Cristobal, has many of the attributes of the standard hero: he is arrogant at times and has a quick temper, he is a philanderer and breaks many hearts in the time-honored tradition, but he is also funny and terribly sweet. If he were alive today instead of in the eighteenth century, he could be taught to accept feminist doctrines to some extent, although he would not be caught dead marching for them. He is also, unlike most heroes, demonstrably smart. Before the death of his father in Madrid recalled him from his studies at Oxford University, he was the joy of his tutors. Most of his faults can be attributed to his youth, for Cristobal is no more than twenty-five. Clare smiles tenderly. It seems strange to her that her readers, many of them ladies twice that age, confer such awesome powers on the boys who stalk through the pages of her books, intent on ravishing.

That, of course, is the problem. Cristobal's youth. Clare is far too old for him. In real life, she knows that young men are very much drawn to her, and she has sampled a few, but a young man of Cristobal's beauty, accomplishments, and aristocratic lineage must have a proper true love. She will not settle for being a one-night stand, no matter how tempting the idea might be, and thus in her fantasies she rewards him with a perfect mate, his beloved Philomena.

Leaning against the paper-towel container, reluctant to return to the company of people less marvelous than Cristobal, she pictures the lovers riding off across the meadow on the Arabian stallion. Philomena rides in front, leaning her head on Cristobal's bosom. One of his hands grasps the reins lightly, for the horse is walking now, gently picking its way through dappled sunlight, carrying its precious cargo off to further amorous adventures. Cristobal's left arm tenderly encircles his love, keeping her close to him. His hand lies against her heart, and from time to time he presses his lips to her bright hair. They are so beautiful and young, the lovers, that Clare is dazzled by their radiance and feels herself on the brink of tears. She must do something about it, bring herself back from her fantasy world before she returns to the others.

Clare has never written on a wall in her life, but now she roots about for her felt-tipped marker with a mission in mind. Considerately, she goes inside the stall where she has seen other names inscribed and, bending down, finds a discreet, clean field. Laughing softly, she begins to stroke the first letter—*C*. She is about to add the *l* when she is overcome by panic. In her drunken state, she had been about to write her own name; lucky that Cristobal's name begins with the same letter, because she can turn the *l* into an *r* and all will be well. Imagine if she had written *Clare & Cristobal* in indelible marker and McCloy, swabbing down the walls in a vain effort to remove the graffiti, had seen it! The thought actually makes her blush, and she works quickly and furtively to complete her task. *Cristobal & Philomena* now blooms on the wall with Mick, Johnny, Angelo, Mary, Sheila, Bernie, and the rest. Through sheer accident, Clare has placed the man's name first, and kept the faith of lavatory romancers.

She is quite eager to leave the scene of the crime and understands that she has performed an irreversible act. It is one thing to sit alone in her kitchen late at night and spin out stories about a man who exists only in her imagination, to invent and reinvent him for her own pleasure, to judge other, mortal, men by the impossibly high standards she has created—it is quite another to write his name on a lavatory wall. There are two stalls in this ladies' room, and Clare knows she will never enter this one again.

Clare has envisioned many ends to her life, some gratifyingly glorious, others (equally) gratifyingly tragic. She has often thought madness might be waiting in the wings; together with every writer she has ever known, the idea of going bonkers is one she accepts with resignation. Until now she has never thought of the madness as some special, comical variety of insanity endemic to those who write historical romances for a living. It is possible that scores of such writers are even now locked up in sanatoriums throughout the world, impervious to the blandishments of sympathetic psychiatrists who do not understand the nature of their madness. It is not an illness likely to be studied by sociologists, since those who suffer from it will never tell. Torture itself would not wring from Clare her secret; it is far too embarrassing.

She leaves the ladies' room and makes her way back to the table. She is trying to prepare an amusing comment, an explanation for her long absence, but nobody seems to have noticed. Far away, lost to her in shadow, Eugene is finding salvation in a Sony Walkman. The place seems dim and deserted to her, sad and full of ghosts.

"We were talking about the annual award for heroism," says Sigrid.

"Now that there are only four of us, it seems a bit pointless," says Joseph.

"I don't know," says Clare, her words popping out unbidden. "I think I am no longer the heroine of my own life."

17

The T. J. Sperling Award

"Someone should tell Gene the phone is ringing."

"Let him be."

"But it might be important."

Sigrid watches while Joseph and Clare debate the problem of the ringing telephone.

"He can't hear with that thing on."

"I always can. You can hear the phone ringing."

"Maybe he has the volume on the highest it can go."

"For Christ's sake," grumbles Douglas, "I'll answer it myself."

Sigrid can taste the vodka in the drink Douglas has made for her, and knows it is much stronger than Clare's drink, which she took the liberty of sampling while Clare was in the ladies'. When she was a teenager she assumed that any boy who tried to ply her with drink was bent on seduction, and she was always right. Douglas, she knows, has mixed her this lethal Bloody Mary because he hopes she will become drunk and reveal more of herself than usual. What he doesn't understand is that by the time it happens, he himself will be so drunk he will neither understand the revelations nor remember them in the morning.

Douglas slams down the phone in disgust and comes toward them shaking his head.

"Who was it?" asks Clare.

"Just some madwoman. A wrong number."

"How do you know she was a madwoman?" asks Clare with great interest.

"She didn't even identify herself, just started right in ranting—something about a lack of consideration. I told her to dial correctly in the future and she cursed me with awesome fury. She said I had no goddamned consideration and she was all alone and what was to prevent her from sticking her head in the fucking oven and ending it once and for all?"

"How extraordinary," says Sigrid. "And you hung up on her?"

"I told her to call Suicide Prevention and *then* I hung up. What else was I supposed to do?"

"Quite right," says Sigrid. "Back to the annual award."

They have been discussing the T. J. Sperling Prize for Most Prolific Hack of the Year, which, for some reason none of them can recall, is always awarded on the first Tuesday they lunch in April. The honorarium goes to the writer who has completed the most manuscripts in the year past, and in former years it had always been a sufficient amount of money for the winner to buy himself a really good lunch or several hardcover books. As Joseph has sadly pointed out, now that they are only four it seems rather pointless.

"Maybe we should each kick in ten dollars instead of five," suggests Sigrid. As last year's Sperling recipient, she knows how depressing it is to be awarded fifteen dollars. No one takes her up on this suggestion. "Let's tally up, then," she says. "Douglas?"

The muscle in Douglas' cheek jumps frantically. "Counting the Irish saga, which will be completed in a few days, only two. I'm not in the running even."

"Three," says Joseph. "Two Hawks and that Gothic for kids."

"Four for me," says Clare. "Volume Two of *The Lundquists,* the contemporary romance about the woman surgeon, and two rippers. I suppose you've won again, Sig?"

"I believe we have a tie," says Sigrid. "As you all know, I ghosted *Medical Miracles,* which, with three romances, brings me up to four, too. I move that the T. J. Sperling prize be awarded to Clare, since I got it last year. Everybody remember to bring an extra five."

"Don't spend it all at once, Clare," says Douglas.

"It must have been nice when there were enough of you to cough up fifty," says Sigrid.

"What a sad group we are," says Clare. "T. J. Sperling would have been ashamed of us. How many books did he write, Douglas? Over a hundred, wasn't it?"

"A hundred and eleven," replies Douglas. "I only met him once, you know. He was at the first hack's lunch I ever attended, along with Frier. Nice old guy, as I recall. He'd worked himself up to the point where he could do a book a month. Twelve a year. He had eight pen names."

"What happened to him?" asks Clare, who knows perfectly well. Sigrid thinks Clare looks like a child who begs to hear a fairy tale she knows by heart.

"He died," says Douglas. "Right at his typewriter. It wasn't long after I'd met him. I was shocked to find out he was only fifty-three. He looked much older."

"No wonder," says Sigrid, shuddering. "A hundred and eleven books. Horrible."

"Heroic," says Joseph. "Here's to him. Here's to T. J. Sperling!"

Douglas drinks laconically. "Of course," he tells them, "the market was better in those days, healthier. You didn't make much, but your dollar went further."

Sigrid thinks Douglas sounds exactly like her father, who made her childhood a misery of boredom by always recalling exactly how little things had cost when he was young. "What would fifteen dollars buy?" she prods, but Douglas ignores her.

"Also, you have to remember the books were shorter then. My Slatts series ran to three hundred pages, maximum, in manuscript form. The bloody Irish saga is coming in at four hundred fifty a volume."

"Still," says Joseph reverently, "T. J. Sperling was a hero."

Sigrid computes the number of novels and other books she has written since becoming a hack five years ago. It comes to fourteen, if she includes her one sally into pornography, *Cherry Pie,* of which the others know nothing. The idea of writing twelve books a year is so repugnant to her that she almost wishes she had not accepted the Sperling Award last April. She has set herself a limit: twenty books. If she is still writing for hire after she has sold twenty books she will consider herself a misfit, a failure, a candidate for the firing squad. She has a master plan which she expects to implement sometime before her thirtieth birthday. With the royalties she has squirreled away from three of her most surprisingly successful books (*Cherry Pie* is one of them, although she had to persuade a lawyer to convince the publisher to send her a proper accounting of what had become an underground classic), she plans to remove herself from New York and settle in Europe. By living frugally, Sigrid has been able to save enough money to cushion her for a full year in some European capital. She knows it is not easy to find work as a waitress or shopgirl without the proper card, and since she plans to make a marriage of convenience in France or Italy or England and secure citizenship, she needs her bankroll to fall back on. If she pulls up stakes now, she will live miserably; in another year or two, with a few more Fionas under her belt, she will be able to manage better. Even considering inflation, and the instability of the economy.

"I don't want to die at my typewriter," she says vehemently. "I don't consider that heroic."

The phone rings again, and Douglas looks at it with loathing. "I think I'll just take it off the hook," he says.

"I'll answer it this time," says Sigrid. She rises and walks with admirable precision toward the bar. She slides under the hatch, as she has seen Gene and Douglas do, and lifts the instrument from its cradle. "Eugene's," she says crisply.

"Who the hell are you?" The voice is slurred and angry.

"This is Sigrid Ericson. Mr. McCloy is engaged at the moment. May I help you?"

"No consideration," growls the voice. "You've got to think of others. Got to fucking think of someone besides your fucking self. Shouldn't get whores to do your dirty work, answer the phone for you. That dirty what's-his-name insulted me before. Told me to call the Suicide Prevention, God rot his brain."

"Madam," says Sigrid, "you have the wrong number. This is McCloy's Saloon. Eugene's. Kindly dial again." She hangs up and then, sensing that the caller will pick out the same number again, waits by the phone. When it rings again she simply lifts the cradle half an inch and replaces it. She repeats this process twice more until she is satisfied that the caller will not try again.

"Who was it?" asks Clare.

"The same madwoman," Sigrid tells her, sliding into her chair.

"One hundred and eleven books," Joey is repeating with inebriated solemnity. "Just imagine it."

"I would really rather not," says Sigrid. "It makes me feel ill."

"I would rather," announces Clare, "spend one hundred and eleven years writing one book." She is so far out of it now, Sigrid sees, that her eyes are nearly crossed.

Sigrid looks around the table at her comrades and feels a vast pity. Ill fortune, bad timing, economic pressures have conspired to place them in a position she is planning to vacate as quickly as possible. Still, each of the others nurses some delusion she knows she would never be capable of harboring. Douglas, particularly, believes himself to be a writer—didn't he quit a profitable job to pursue it full-time? Joey is a failed academic, whose doctoral thesis on Christopher Marlowe has convinced him that he will be able to wring nobility from his typewriter and cover himself with honor sometime in the future. Clare, with the hyperbolic and fervid imagination of the one-time actress, throws herself at the typewriter with the same self-destructive sexual energy Sigrid has seen her exhibit in bit parts on the "Late, Late Show."

Only Sigrid understands that she writes because it is something she can do well. It is an odd talent, like being able to juggle pumpkins or tap out tunes on water glasses; she has not asked for this talent, any more than a freak asks for his deformity, and yet it is there. She has simply gone to her proper place, just as a woman with two noses or a man with the skin of a crocodile seeks employment in a freak show, but unlike these unfortunates she can eventually leave and seek her place in the real world. Douglas, Clare, and Joseph, she thinks, have forgotten that another world exists.

"Hey," she says kindly, "drink up. We should leave now. It's getting late."

18

Giving Comfort

Rather than think of his son's body beneath the wheels of a bus, McCloy has been giving himself up to the music. There is a technique to it, this abandon, and he has made several errors before getting it right. The tape Joey has put in for him is full of tricks; just when you've heard something rollicking and cheerful, the composer stops short and introduces you to sweet, sorrowful stuff that lands you right back where you didn't want to be.

McCloy is not by nature given to self-pity, but Sigrid's question, the newspaper account, the unnaturally mournful tenor of the day have set him to thinking morbidly. When he is caught off-guard by the violins he is angry at first. He does not know that the composer is evoking winter, nor can he know that Joseph has recorded the *Four Seasons* out of sequence for his own reasons. He has been plunged from spring to winter without the appropriate connecting seasons to prepare him, but he doesn't know that, either. He only stands and accepts what the machine gives him, and gradually he is caught up in the beauty of it. The faces of Tim and Pat still hover dangerously close, and once the face of the bus driver, poor man, who wept like an inconsolable little boy. He had not been at fault. Each year, on the anniversary of Tim's death, he sends flowers to Mr. and Mrs. Eugene McCloy at their old address. This seems to

McCloy a curiously inappropriate gesture, but he understands that the bus driver wants him to know he will never forget. He hopes the parents of the dead boy will derive some comfort from the knowledge that his life, too, will never be the same. Even though McCloy no longer lives in the same house, the flowers come unerringly to him every sixth day of June; he keeps the card, which is signed with the bus driver's name, and tells Nora to take the flowers to her church for an altar decoration. He has nine cards neatly stacked in the top drawer of his bureau, each inscribed with the name "Walter P. Buchanan." Soon he will have ten.

Mr. Buchanan has no way of knowing that Mrs. McCloy has not lived in the house in Queens for some years now. Patricia has removed herself to the Southwest, which seems to suit her. She moves around a lot, from Santa Fe to Phoenix to Abilene to Albuquerque, sending occasional postcards or brief notes to McCloy. In the last of these the name on the return address was neither his nor her own maiden name, but one unknown to him, so he supposes she is now someone's common-law wife. She has never asked him for a divorce and probably never will—since she cannot have any more children, why bother to marry?

Nora can be roused to excesses of venom on the subject of Pat, whom she considers heartless, whorish, self-centered, and disloyal. A deserter, like Nora's husband Brendan. McCloy has forbidden her to ransack Tim's memory, but he knows Nora must have some outlet for her rages; it is better to have her rant against a world in which Pat and Brendan can be permitted to exist than to have her weep over a world in which Tim was allowed such a brief inhabitance. Better for him.

While the elegiac beauty of winter music streams from the earphones, McCloy's thoughts dart helplessly back to the very images he had hoped to banish. Here is Pat, wearing her ice-blue nylon nightie, chain-smoking in the kitchen at four in the morning. Before her is a bottle of Seagram's V.O., which she does not like, being a drinker of beer or rosé wine, but which she has taken to drinking lately because she has faith in its ability to dull her senses. Her face is haggard, remote. She barely acknowledges his presence, but merely lights one cigarette from the butt of another. Her feet are propped up on the table, which causes the nightie to slip down her fine, long thighs and reveal the tender juncture where rust-colored pubic hairs curl in a frolicsome way. Tim has been dead for six months. The room is full of the sharp, feral odor of Pat's unwashed body. She has only one thing to say to him, when he approaches, intent on comforting and saving her. "You were asleep," she says tonelessly. It is an accusation: just as she claimed greater ownership of Tim when he was alive, now she claims the sole right to grieve for him. McCloy's pain is of no consequence, placed next to hers; on a Richter Scale of grief, his is puny, hers monumental, shattering all known records. It is an attitude she will never abandon, as it turns out. She cannot help it, any more than the bus driver could avoid crushing the child who ran out so carelessly into his path. Pat cannot escape her nature any more than Walter P. Buchanan, or Tim, could avoid their fates. And so McCloy loses both wife and child in one blow—his fate—and since Nora has been deserted by the feckless Brendan, it seems only natural for them to consolidate their two sad households into one. He will always be responsible for Nora now, just as, when they were children in County Clare, she was responsible for him. That is the way life works.

The brasses of summer bring him some relief. This seesawing of emotions reminds him of an old record his father used to play on the gramophone back home—*Paddy Brannon & The Kerry Boys, Their Greatest Hits,* it was called—in which lively jigs and reels were juxtaposed with haunting laments, so you never knew how to feel at all. Perhaps this composer, like Paddy Brannon, was obliged to collect all his greatest hits on one record and was only trying for variety. McCloy thinks he will soon purchase a Walkman and ask Joseph how he can obtain this fine tune playing at present without having the mournful one, lovely though it may be.

When the music comes to an end with a little click, he considers turning the cassette over, but a glance at the clock tells him it is nearly half-past five. He should have known, since some time ago he observed Maxine locking the riot-gates to the hosiery store, but he is astounded at this passage of time. He switches on some lights above the bar and notices the phone's receiver has not been properly replaced. A tinny siren has been wailing away to alert him to this fact. He replaces the receiver and looks toward the back room.

"Everything alright, then?" he calls. The hacks, who have been slumping dejectedly, straighten up and smile at him. They look very much less presentable than they did on arriving; even Sigrid has lost some of her newly minted crispness. McCloy cannot understand why they are still sitting about and searches for the right words to express his confusion without seeming inhospitable. He comes out from behind the bar to return Joseph's Walkman.

"Having a special celebration?" he asks, laying the machine on the table and touching Joey's shoulder in thanks.

"We are drinking the health of the winner of the T. J. Sperling Award," says Douglas.

"That's me," says Clare. "Actually, we were saying we should go home, but now it's the rush hour. Couldn't bear it."

"If you wouldn't mind," says Joseph, "we could just stay until the worst of it is over. We wouldn't be any trouble."

The lad sounds like a refugee. "Mind?" says McCloy. "Why would I mind?" Normally, he would serve up a round on the house in honor of Clare's award, whatever it might be, but he thinks they have had enough. "I could make you all some coffee," he says. "Fresh coffee."

"Perhaps another drink," says Clare vaguely.

Suddenly, they are all talking at once. Douglas wants him to know he has kept an accounting of drinks he has made while McCloy was otherwise occupied. It is written on a napkin somewhere. Sigrid is telling him of a series of wrong-number phone calls. Joseph, who is for some reason speaking with an English accent now, is repeating that McCloy is a prince of a fellow. Clare is ordering a final round of drinks. "At this stage," she says, "one can only go forward, don't you think?"

Distressingly, Clare leaps up to help him when he moves to take their glasses. She is intent on emptying the ashtrays, as if she were a guest in his house. She bumps against him, apologizes. "There's no need, Clare. Just sit and enjoy yourself." But Clare insists on helping.

"I'm *not* enjoying myself," she says to him when he is back behind the bar. "This has been a terrible afternoon, Gene." She is almost whimpering, like a little girl whose scoop of ice cream has plunged from the cone into a pile of dust.

"Now, Clare," he says, wondering what has happened to the Tabasco sauce, "that can't be true. Tell me about this grand award you've won. It sounds most impressive."

"It's just a joke. I've written more trash than the others this year. I've won fifteen dollars for helping more trees to die."

The name Sperling leaps into its proper slot. "Ah," says McCloy, "I thought the name was familiar. When I first took over the place, Mr. Sperling used to drop in with that fella you censured. T. J. Sperling—Tom, he was. A nice old party."

"He wasn't all that old," says Clare, who is almost wailing now. "He died in harness, Gene. One hundred and eleven books."

"Could you make that a double?" bellows Douglas from the back room.

McCloy calls that the drinks are on the house, and makes very weak ones all around. Clare is resting her curly head on the bar. "I wish I could have a job here," she says dreamily. "I would wear my glasses when I poured the shots. I would even clean the lavatories."

Horrified, McCloy pats her hand. It is the first time he has ever touched her, and he feels that he has committed an indiscretion. "I don't think it would suit you, Clare. You already have a fine profession. You weren't cut out to be a barmaid."

Clare imprisons his hand and holds it fiercely. "You're such a nice man, Gene. We all love you, you know."

McCloy feels his face go red with embarrassment at this effusion, yet it is far from unpleasant to have Clare hold his hand, especially when she relaxes her grip a bit. Here is a woman, he thinks, who would not reject comfort. Her head is still resting on the bar, her lips are only inches from their two hands. He can feel her warm breath against his wrist. He thinks of the stuff she writes. How is it possible for such a gentle creature to imagine such things?

While he is struggling to frame a reply, the door opens and Mr. and Mrs. Ryan stump in for their early drinks. Ryan is a retired police officer, and he and his wife like to down several before continuing on their mysterious evening rounds.

"Hey, Yew-geen!" cries Mrs. Ryan merrily, "This weather's not for shit, huh?"

"Be right with you," says McCloy.

"I'll take the drinks to the table, if you'll give me a tray," says Clare.

"Ya got a new employee, Yew-geen?"

His real evening has begun.

19

An Exorcism

Joseph is feeling guilty about keeping his secret to himself and wants to atone. He forgets that Douglas, even in his present state, will catch him out, and offers them a much lesser secret instead.

"I hit bottom," he says cheerfully. "I wrote a film strip."

"A film script? I hope you were tremendously well paid," says Sigrid.

"A film *strip*. They're audiovisual aids. Nobody moves in them until they advance the strip."

"Are they pornographic?"

"God no, Sig. They're for children in schools."

"I know what he means," says Clare. "I wrote one once, ages ago. It was about understanding your parents' divorce. You make up dismal situations and write the dialogue and voice-over, and then they photograph people and put it all together."

"That's basically it," says Joseph. Mine wasn't so dramatic, though. It was called 'Meet Your Congressperson.' 'Representative Frank Enslow's busy day starts at five A.M., when he rises to read position papers before dawn. It is not unusual for Congressman Enslow to put in eighteen hours a day serving the people who have elected him to the House of Representatives.' That kind of thing. I had to do a woman, too, for equal time."

"What was her name?" asks Clare.

"Never mind her," says Sigrid. "I like Congressman Frank Enslow better. What a name! So patrician. Do you show him in the tidal basin with hookers at the end of his busy day?"

"I owed two months rent, and they offered me two thou. It seemed like simple work and I needed the money." Joseph spreads his hands and smiles sheepishly. "Hardest thing I ever had to write."

"Factual things are always harder," says Sigrid.

"I kept picturing the shot they'd do, and wondering how I could fit everything around that one picture. When I wrote this scene with Congressman Enslow in his office, greeting his constituents, all I could see was how his lips wouldn't move when he talked. And the constituents! There'd be maybe six lines of dialogue and *nobody's lips would move.*"

"How depressing," says Sigrid. "Still, you paid your rent. Is it still so low?"

Joseph nods, aware of their envy. He pays under four hundred dollars for his apartment in Brooklyn, which is quite roomy by Manhattan standards. Sigrid pays that much as an illegal sublessee in what she has described as a closet with a window; Clare and Douglas pay vastly more.

"I'm so afraid my apartment will go co-op," says Clare. "What will I do if it happens? Go to the Women's Shelter?"

"Well, it was an experience," says Joseph. "They paid very promptly, I will say that. Of course I'm broke again—I bought the Walkman and these Tony Lama boots. One thing and another, it just goes." He does not mention the case of very nice wine he has purchased on a whim. It is not wine meant to be drunk alone. He has only slept with three women since Vivvy's departure, and each of these events took place on the lady's home turf.

"Oh, look," says Clare. "The television's on. It's the six o'clock news."

Joseph obediently looks. None of them has ever seen the TV turned on in Eugene's before. "There are half a dozen people at the bar," he says. "When did they come in?"

"It's the evening trade," says Douglas. It is the first time he has spoken since Joseph mentioned the film strip. "Did you think Gene survived by giving us lunch and a few drinks every other Tuesday? In a few hours this bar will be packed." He is smiling knowingly, making Joseph uneasy. *Wrong secret,* he seems to be saying.

"So I wrote a film strip," says Joseph. "What are you going to do—censure me?"

"I would never censure a man for doing an honest day's work to earn his bread." He stresses the word "honest."

Clare and Sigrid have become very girlish, watching the evening news together. Clare has put her glasses on, and the two of them are running a constant commentary on the figures who appear on the screen. They talk back to Reagan, tell the anchorman to find a new barber.

"If he'd *thin* his hair," Clare murmurs. "Few people need that done, but he would definitely benefit."

A picture of the Capitol Building appears and both of them shriek: "We want Congressman Frank Enslow!"

"Enslow for President!"

"The Writers' Liberation Army throws its full support behind the candidacy of Frank Enslow—a man who cares!"

"Girls will be girls," says Douglas. "Even Sigrid seems to be feeling the effects of an afternoon's debauch." He is still staring smilingly at Joseph, daring him to make the real confession. Joseph feels cold to the tips of his fingers now. He thinks he is like a tourist on a Caribbean island who unwittingly blunders into a revolution and ends up in a cell, faced with a merciless interrogator. He can remain silent, innocent by virtue of his silence, and let Douglas torture him, or he can confess and bring the final havoc down on his head. In his case not the firing squad, but ridicule.

"Oh dear," says Clare. She removes her glasses and stops watching the news.

"What is it?"

"A case of child abuse. Awful."

"I sometimes think," says Sigrid, "that people abuse their children so they can appear on television when they're arrested."

Douglas raps for attention, his fist nearly missing the table and pounding his own knee. "Joseph has something to tell us," he says. "He has an announcement to make. A confession."

"You shit," says Joseph. "You storm trooper."

"For his own good." Douglas turns to Joseph paternally. "This will hurt me more than it does you, but it's for your own good."

"Sadist," says Joseph. "Gestapo."

"What is it?" asks Sigrid. "Are you getting re-married?"

"If you're so all-knowing," says Joseph to his tormentor, "tell my secret yourself. Let's see how good you are at inventing other people's lives."

"You're on." Douglas takes a large sip of his drink, shudders all over like a damp dog, and begins. "Joseph has fallen prey to the most dangerous delusion writers like ourselves can harbor. It is not his fault. Poverty, lack of recognition, humiliation, loneliness, great personal loss of an emasculating sort, fears for the future, doubts about the present, a revisionary view of the past—all these have combined to lower his immunity. Joey is the most fertile of fields just now. He is like a rich loam into which the seeds of delusion may be dropped with optimum results."

"Douglas gets terribly articulate when he has too much to drink," says Clare.

"Quiet, Clare. This is serious business. We must band together to exorcise Joey of these demons. It's a painful business, disabusing him of the very idea which allows him to experience some happiness, but we have no choice. He may call me a sadist, but I am, at heart, one who detests giving pain. The only thing I hate more is standing by like a coward, doing nothing, while someone I like flounders in the arms of demonic delusion."

"What *is* Douglas talking about?" whispers Clare to Sigrid.

"The pain will be much greater further down the road," continues Douglas, "and if I must sting Joey now to prevent it, I will. It is better than watching him writhe in agony later on."

"What *are* you talking about, Douglas?"

"Joseph"—Douglas pauses dramatically—"is writing what he thinks is a real novel. No doubt it is autobiographical. He believes it is literature, he looks forward to the time when reviewers will hail him as the find of the year, he imagines the plaudits and kudos he will receive. Perhaps he goes so far as to draft his acceptance speech at the National Book Awards. At any rate, he is in great danger. Because certain events have occurred to him in his life so far, and because he has a certain facility for writing, he imagines he can combine the two and emerge a literary hero."

Joseph is sitting well back in his chair, trying to appear tolerant at this (quite accurate) dissection of his current state of mind. He is stunned at Douglas' ability to see into his innermost thoughts and turn his dream to rubbish in a few words. Douglas has it all right, even down to the autobiographical aspect of the novel.

"Is this true, Joey?" Clare speaks very gently.

"I don't know why you bother to ask me," he says. "Douglas is the one who knows it all."

"Oh, you mustn't," says Clare. "Give it up now, before it's too late."

"Listen to Clare," says Douglas. "She knows."

"Nobody will want to buy it, Joey dear. All that work and personal angst, all those lovely words, and pages and pages of stuff you could weep over late at night! Nobody wants to read them, Joey. You'll only break your heart. I have one at home, five hundred pages it is, at the bottom of a cedar chest."

"Did you try to sell it?" asks Sigrid.

"Oh my, yes. I have seventeen rejection slips. I think of it rather like a dead baby, you know?"

"You see," says Douglas, "we've all been there. We're only trying to help. I have one too."

"It's not that they're not well written, these books," says Clare, speaking as if unsold autobiographical novels form a huge sub-genre, "but unless you're a genius, why would anyone want to read about your life?"

"Well, suppose you were a lion tamer or a famous courtesan?" asks Sigrid.

"Don't be so unfeeling, Sig," says Clare. "You know we're not discussing celebrity autobiographies."

"You see?" Douglas touches Joey's arm in comradely fashion. "I told you—we've all been there."

"Not me," says Sigrid. "I can't imagine wanting to write about myself. I don't see why Joey shouldn't give it a shot, though. You're jealous, that's all."

Joseph thinks it is like being de-programmed, or urged to agree to a plea bargain. Sigrid, an improbable ally, is playing the part of good cop, while Clare and Douglas—under their gentle, sorrowful demeanors—are the bad guys. They don't want him to succeed. He feels trapped in a nightmare, and refuses to speak. Douglas' hand still lies heavy on his sleeve; Clare's dark eyes are brimming sympathy from across the table. Nobody answers Sigrid's charge.

"Please, Joey," Clare whispers. "Give it up while there's still time. Trust me."

"For your own good, Joey," says Douglas.

20

Strumpets

Sigrid and Clare sit alone together at the table in the back room. Joseph is still with them, but his presence doesn't count, for he is wearing his Walkman. Ever since the discussion about his autobiographical novel, he has refused to speak.

"What's happening at the bar?" Clare asks.

"Douglas is trying to blend in with the clientele. He's cocking his leg on the bar-rail and trading remarks with the others, but mostly they're ignoring him. I think he went off because he was guilty about Joey."

"He shouldn't be, you know. He was quite right."

Both cast an eye at Joseph worriedly, but he seems quite happy; he pulls at his beer and makes the odd remark to himself in a loud but unintelligable voice.

"What else?" asks Clare.

"Well, there are about twenty people now. Some of them look wet, so I suppose it's sleeting again. Eugene is very busy—he has a whole new personality—and there's another barman helping him. He's a youngish man, very muscular, with a drooping mustache and mean eyes and a nice smile."

"What about Gene's new personality?"

"Honestly, Clare, if you don't like your glasses, why don't you get contact lenses?"

"I had a scare with those," says Clare. "Once, when I was working to a deadline—I think it was a Regency—I sat at my typewriter for eighteen hours straight. I ended up with a corneal abrasion, absolutely hellish. I couldn't see and I couldn't cry and it hurt like anything. It's odd, because when you think of the health hazards connected to writing, you always picture a collapsed lung from chain-smoking, or some weird personality disorder stemming from too much solitude. Whoever would imagine a corneal abrasion?"

"I'll play your game," says Sigrid. "I'll be your eyes. Gene's new personality, new to us, is one of great *authority.* I think we intimidate him. At night, he is absolute master."

"Are his lips curved in a mocking smile? Do the steely muscles in his thighs ripple as he strides, pantherlike, to the Guinness tap?"

"Not exactly, Clare." Sigrid inclines her head, wishing to please this woman who falls midway between those she could envy and those she is forced to respect, and whispers thrillingly, "He feels her presence in every fiber of his being. The dark eyes, great pools of night, seem to impale him as he goes about his work. Cords of muscles stand up along his powerful arms when he pulls the tap. His eyes gleam sardonically as he mutters, 'Damn you, Lady Clare—damn you for a taunting strumpet of a hell-cat!"

"Oh, wonderful!" cries Clare. "I'd forgotten all about the word 'strumpet.' It's so necessary, don't you think? It sounds like something on the menu for high tea. A strawberry crumpet."

"I always thought it sounded like a thing you'd feed to livestock. 'Mix a little strumpet in her feed and that heifer will be right as rain,' said the kindly old vet to the worried farmer." Clare looks enchanted, as if Sigrid has imparted something of value.

"Your father was a farmer, wasn't he?" Clare says.

This is a tricky moment. Sigrid cannot remember if she has told the group that she comes from farming stock. It is one of her favorite replies when people ask what her family did, back in Wisconsin or Minnesota or Kansas, all these states seeming part of one vast field to the eastern mind. Clare is from the Pacific northwest, though, and might actually have some knowledge of farming, even if she is a judge's daughter. Sigrid has a brief, uncharacteristic desire to tell Clare the unvarnished truth, but she can't risk contradicting herself.

"Yes, yes," she says humorously, "lots and lots of dreary soybeans and such. Rising before dawn; to bed with the chickens. Hired man named Olaf. Bloody accidents involving the combine harvester."

"I've often wondered why you write so movingly about the land," says Clare. "Now I know. You were a part of it."

"Oh, but I hated it!" says Sigrid. "All that flat, sad land, stretching away to nowhere! The isolation, the lack of thought, the general feeling that any conversation not pertaining to the weather or your neighbors' indiscretions was somehow—*frivolous.* Peculiar! Any hint of eccentricity was treated as a sign of mental illness there. If you showed the slightest sign of wanting to get away, make a life somewhere else, they laughed at you."

"But that was the people," says Clare, adding fatuously, "the land is very different. The land is not responsible for the people who settle it."

Sigrid considers for the hundredth time the complex rules for lying successfully, and decides she has not been remiss. Her cardinal rule—one always transplants the locale into the proper emotional soil and one cannot go wrong—has not been violated. All she has said of the people and prevailing social codes of her childhood is correct; only the scene has been changed. Sigrid is the oldest child and only daughter of a Detroit policeman and his wife; her mother is the sort of woman for whom the highest artistic endeavor is fixing seashells to bathroom glasses by means of epoxy bond. She has three younger brothers, ranging in age from nineteen to twenty-six. The eldest of these is engaged in the carpet-shampooing business, the middle one is studying to be a Lutheran minister, and the baby of the family is in jail for the possession and sale of narcotics, last she heard. The closest she has ever come to the land, as Clare calls it, is a Fresh Air camp in northern Wisconsin, where she was deported at the age of nine on account of a lingering bronchitis. Sigrid is not fond of the outdoors and thinks its proper place is between the pages of a book, where it is made to seem so much nicer than it really is.

"Aren't you ever tempted to go back for class reunions?" asks Clare. "Aren't you curious?"

"My school was quite rural," says Sigrid, quickly imagining a little frame schoolhouse at the edge of a cornfield. The students would wear bib overalls and be excused early for chores during harvest and planting times. "There were only about four kids my age. We don't have reunions."

Clare shudders. "This summer is my twentieth reunion," she says morosely. "Imagine. Two of my graduating class have already died of natural causes. My mother always phones to tell me."

Sigrid wants to lead Clare out of her melancholy and looks toward the bar for distraction. The new barman is answering the phone. He speaks into the instrument, winces, holds it at some distance from his ear. Then he calls McCloy to the phone. "Gene is talking to someone on the telephone," she tells Clare. "He's sort of hunched up, talking, as if he wants privacy. Do you suppose it's his mistress?"

"Why not his wife?" Clare is offended for Gene's sake. "I don't think he would cheat on his wife."

"How do you know he's married?"

"Joey said his wife's name was Nora."

Clare's voice has taken on the misty, tender note it assumes when she discusses McCloy. Sigrid wonders if Clare's sentimentalization of McCloy is more serious than she has believed. Perhaps Clare is suffering from a dangerous romantic delusion. She may think of McCloy as a sort of noble savage, a man like Lady Chatterley's lover, capable of rising to poetic grandeur during the act of love. Sigrid looks at Gene's narrow back, his thinning hair, and sees nothing of potential erotic value, but then, she does not much care for sex and might not be able to tell.

"I think Gene is secretly pining for you," she tells Clare. "You're his favorite."

"Don't be silly, Sig," says Clare. Her voice is sharp, but she seems to blush.

"Think what it would do for him if you took him on."

"You make us sound like boxers."

"It might be quite gratifying." Sigrid knows it can be pleasant to have affairs with plain, simple men, because they are so stunned and grateful. They are so overwhelmed at being singled out, they fail to pick quarrels and ask embarrassing questions; unlike their flashier, more splendid competitors, they do not batter you with their bodies and then spend endless hours asking how you liked it. They are gentle, kind, considerate, awed at their good fortune, and anxious to preserve the status quo. Sigrid thinks it would do Clare good to indulge in such an affair. They have never confided intimacies to one another, but Sigrid is sure Clare goes for the steely-thighed, sardonic types she writes about. Even though she calls her last husband "the Leech," he was, as she always assures the group, a very handsome man.

"It wouldn't necessarily have to be Eugene," she explains. "It could be anyone decent and without a hint of glamour or ego. A high school math teacher, your accountant, the man who mends your boots—someone like that."

Clare giggles. "None of those, thanks. I do see what you mean, Sig, and it's nice of you to take an interest, but I have my hands full at the moment. As it were." She laughs out loud now, dips her head, laughs again. "I wish I could pass him along to you," she whinnies. "You'd know how to handle him."

"If he's handsome and witty and vain, I don't want him."

"That's exactly what he is," says Clare, nodding manically. "That's my Chris." She laughs again. "A real bastard. Charming, though."

Sigrid is alarmed, both by Clare's near-hysteria and by the feeling that Clare's laughter is partly directed at her. Clare may be assuming that she is naive and rustic, a sort of sexual yokel used only to coupling with farmhands. In her large-breasted, confident way, Clare is being condescending. That is the trouble with lying creatively, inventing yourself, telling people what you know will most please them, what best fits their picture of you; in their arrogance, they elbow you away and finish writing your story themselves. It is a nasty habit, and greedy, this wheedling for the plot without proper attention to subtlety. She would not have suspected Clare of harboring such petty instincts.

Sigrid contemplates a course of education for Clare. While Joseph sits, catatonically insulated by his earphones, she will tell Clare about her baby, whose father was an itinerant musician of middling fame. The child, a girl, was born nine months after Sigrid's disappointing night of passion in a motel room near Ann Arbor, and subsequently adopted by a family whose name Sigrid has never cared to know. How it would surprise Clare to see how much of the maternal instinct is pure myth, and how it would offend her sense of the romantic to learn how little, on balance, the birth of the child has disturbed the flow of Sigrid's life! Besides life itself, Sigrid has given her daughter only one thing, a name: Lily. In a rare moment of sentimentality, Sigrid named the baby for her favorite literary heroine, Lily Bart. Whenever she thinks of Lily, which is seldom, she hopes her daughter will come to a better end than her namesake.

She is forming the beginning sentence of the tale when she sees the futility of educating Clare. It would only be an exercise in cruelty, since Clare is really too old to profit from such a lesson. Let her keep her illusions, since, unlike Joseph's, they are not likely to harm her now.

"Here comes Douglas," she says, cutting short Clare's eccentric, solitary mirth. "He looks perturbed."

"Douglas always looks perturbed," says Clare sourly. "Tell me something new."

"Too late." Sigrid smiles, pleased at the double meaning. "Too late, dear Clare."

Before Douglas can join them, she reaches out and squeezes Clare's arm. It is meant to be a gesture of affection. Women should stick together, if only superficially, in this odd profession of theirs. In the dwindling group of soldiers of fortune, she and Clare are the only women left. If Clare is exhibiting signs of battle fatigue, then, Sigrid thinks, it is her duty to show understanding. She, Sigrid, is a younger soldier, one who plans to retire before years at the typewriter have spoiled her for civilian life; in the meantime she will do her best to aid and comfort those further along in the ranks.

She looks from the weary Clare to the temporarily shell-shocked Joseph, and awaits the return of the mad old Colonel, Douglas, bringing them news from the front.

21

The Wrong Smile

"The madwoman called again," Douglas tells them. His sojourn at the bar has perked him up a bit. It is a matter, he believes, of getting away from the company of his neurotic fellow writers and drinking elbow-to-elbow with members of the decent laboring classes. Steamfitters, policemen, construction workers, plumbers—vaguely, Douglas imagines the customers in McCloy's saloon to be members of these professions. The salt of the earth. "She screamed at Mike for a long time. Called him a would-be assassin."

"Who is Mike?" asks Sigrid.

"The barman. She accused him of conspiring with some low woman to murder her and make it look like a suicide." He leans forward, lowers his voice. "It's all because I told her to call Suicide Prevention," he explains. "She thinks it was Mike."

"And I'm the low woman," says Sigrid.

"Right. She says she called Suicide Prevention and warned them not to fall for any tricks. I could hear the whole thing from two feet away."

"You must learn to be more careful with people," says Clare. "You might have caused great damage, Douglas."

"Gene handled it. He got on the phone and whispered away—very secretive and caressing tones he used—I couldn't hear what he said—and that was that."

"Probably," says Joseph, who has taken off his earphones when no one was looking, "Gene told her his place was temporarily taken over by misfits and lunatics. People who have no reason to be here beyond a certain hour. People who get drunk in the afternoon, instead of when normal people get drunk, because they have nothing better to do. Probably he had to apologize for us. I wish I could have heard what he said."

"Horseshit," says Douglas. The look in Joey's eyes makes him wish he were back at the bar; it is a look of humorous self-loathing that Douglas has never seen there before, a look Douglas often adopts himself. He has always imagined the look, translated in the viewer's vision, to be one of charming cynicism and witty, almost Gallic, world-weariness. He equates the look with certain facets of his writing.

Reville delights in playing cat and mouse with his readers. He delivers the expected emotion on cue, only to snatch it away, holding it up, on further inspection, as a flawed entity—

Entity? No.

—as a piece of business riddled with small pockmarks through which may enter the bracing winds of doubt, followed by a certain knowledge that a veritable typhoon of unpleasant truths will soon engulf the reader—

A typhoon of unpleasant truths? "Small pockmarks" is even worse, "the bracing winds of doubt" the very nadir. He is too drunk to write his own reviews.

He is not too drunk to ignore, in Joseph's expression, a terrifying intimation of his own possible clownishness. Joey seems neither witty nor world-weary, only wounded. In Joseph's carefully articulated speech and self-deprecating smile Douglas sees the device by which all failed men seek to salvage dignity—it is the position of a military commander who has shot all his own men by mistake, or a handkerchief salesman who has failed to meet his quota. Is it possible that he, Douglas, looks like this to others?

"Horseshit," he says again, with less conviction. "Why should Gene apologize for us? We only answered the phone because he was hiding out under your earphones. What were you trying to do, Joe—corrupt the only good bartender left on the Upper West Side?"

"That's right," says Joey, still smiling his tight little smile, "blame me. Turn everything around, the way you always do. You're the kind of man picks a fight and then pretends it was all a joke. You can't exist without offending people—it's your drug; you're addicted to being offensive. The trouble with you, Reville, if anyone ever told you the truth about yourself, you'd fold up like a moth and crumble into a powder. That's why everyone allows you to be such a prick. We don't want to witness the spectacle of a middle-aged guy in tweeds bawling like a baby because somebody finally told him he was a third-rate son of a bitch."

"Oh, Joey," says Clare in shocked tones, "you don't mean that."

"Yes, he does!" cries Douglas jovially. "The worm turns—truthfully! Bravo, Joseph." He claps his hands together, bringing them up to hide the jerking muscle in his cheek, which has executed a sort of polka under Joseph's attack. He has heard this speech before, or versions of it, but always his accusers have been women. He has never had a member of his own sex speak out in such poisonous rage on the subject of his abrasiveness.

It is a part of Reville's technique to bully the reader into accepting the unacceptable. One must admire his willingness to be unlovable; Reville, we feel, is a man who would rather write truthfully in a vacuum than—

"Douglas is not third-rate," says Sigrid. "None of us is first-rate, but we're not third-rate, either."

"Perhaps second-rate," says Clare. "But on a scale of what?"

"I've just insulted you, Reville," says Joseph. "I've told you the truth about yourself, and all you can do is pretend I was joking. Clare and Sigrid are doing their version of a farcical Greek chorus, we can leave them out of this, but just between the two of us—don't you hate what I've just said?"

Douglas considers. In truth, he does smart from Joseph's words, but the feeling is blunted by alcohol; in the future, when he is sober, he suspects he will spend many hours brooding over this incident. He has already proved that he does not crumble to a powder—at least visibly—when attacked, but the words "third-rate" have great power to wound him. The girls know this—they are making a great show of it in order to defuse the bomb. His best course is tolerance.

"Ah, Joey," he says, "you're such a *writer.* Only a writer would ask for a review of his insults. It wasn't a bad speech, all in all."

"Admit it!" Joseph cries. "Didn't you *hate* it?" His voice is loud now; he shouts the words as if encouraging Douglas to challenge him to a duel. The patrons at the bar stop talking and turn curious faces toward the back room. Eugene is regarding them with mild alarm, his hand, in the act of pouring a jigger, held motionless.

Douglas folds his arms across his chest and smiles at his adversary. Joseph seems, suddenly, to be one of his own children—his son, aged seven or eight and desperately anxious to test his strength against the parental authority. Douglas feels tenderness for Joey, and not a little parental guilt. Perhaps he has been too hard on the boy; it is possible that Joseph cannot stand large doses of truth at this critical juncture in his life. Douglas means his smile to be gentle, forbearing, but long years of perfecting a different sort of smile guide his lips into the accustomed pattern. Without knowing it, he appears to be sneering. He is utterly amazed, therefore, when Joseph springs to his feet and lurches toward him, head lowered like a fighting bull.

"Stand up!" he shouts. "On your feet, you fucking fake!"

It happens so quickly that Douglas is caught, hands folded around his midsection, still gazing up at Joseph with bemused eyes, since he thinks it is all a boozy joke. Joseph grasps at the lapels of Douglas' Harris tweed jacket and scrabbles about in a vain effort to drag his enemy to a standing position. Douglas, feeling ridiculous, frees his hands from the warm comfort of his sides and tries to ward off the clutching fingers, and Joseph, cursing loudly, strikes an openhanded blow. It is an awkward blow. It misses its target and glances along the lobe of Douglas' left ear.

At last, Douglas realizes that he is being physically assaulted. He has written about barroom fights many times in his Slatts novels, but, except for a brief scuffle during his sophomore year in college, he has never been a participant. What is he supposed to do? He outweighs Joey by at least forty pounds and cannot imagine striking him.

Joseph is still trying to haul him to his feet. He has stopped uttering a string of curses and works with quiet fury, his expression as determined as it must have been when he was completing his Christopher Marlowe thesis. Dozens of faces are looking on from the front room, Clare has half-risen to her feet, and Sigrid is murmuring something about coffee. Joseph still tugs at his lapels doggedly. This could go on forever.

Douglas rises to his feet so suddenly that Joey's body goes reeling off, propelled backward against the wall. "Come on, Joe," Douglas says kindly. "Enough now." But Joseph lowers his head and rushes forward, fists balled. Douglas raises his own hands in a humorous gesture of surrender and receives a blow in the chest that quite stuns him. No sooner has he recovered—it has only knocked him back a pace—than one of Joey's knobbly fists collides with his lower jaw, causing him to bite his lip painfully.

Joey has retreated now in a little dancing motion; he seems to be shoring up his strength to withstand Douglas's counterattack. Douglas can taste blood in his mouth, and from the corner of his eyes he sees McCloy approaching purposefully. Action is required, quickly, before the situation becomes too humiliating. Joey is hurtling toward him again. Douglas catches the slight arms raised against him and firmly propels Joey backward, trying to put him in his seat again, but Joseph is unexpectedly strong in his anger and refuses to be lowered into his chair. It is an almost impossible task to seat him. Sighing, Douglas lets go of his arms and pushes him firmly downward. Joseph pops up again and Douglas, in despair, places both hands against his chest and thrusts him away as hard as he can.

Clare utters a cry of fright as Joseph flies past his chair, one of his feet knocking several glasses from the table, and lands in a heap against the wall. The only sound is the shattering of glass against the tile and a soft gasp from the figure now recumbent on the floor. The whole incident has taken less than twenty seconds.

"What's this all about?" McCloy's tone is stern for the first time. He approaches Douglas with the neutral authority of a traffic cop. "What's happened here?" he repeats.

Douglas swallows blood and gives a little shrug. "Just a misunderstanding, Gene," he says. "Sorry for the commotion."

McCloy goes to Joey and squats by his side. "Alright, then, Joe?" he asks. Joey's reply is too soft to hear, but he shakes his head several times, as if to clear it, then shambles to his feet and heads for the men's room without a backward look. McCloy casts an odd look in Douglas' direction, but he will not ask for enlightenment. Douglas wants not to lose Eugene's approval, but he cannot say, like a little boy: *He started it.*

It is Sigrid who takes control. "Actually," she says to McCloy,

"Joey started the whole thing. Douglas was just trying to make him sit down."

"Well," says McCloy, "it's been a long day for you. Best drink up and go and get some dinner."

Douglas sees Clare wince and knows that she has heard the directive beneath the kindly words. *Get out, now. You don't belong here at this hour. You are to be here on alternate Tuesdays, between the hours of two and four.*

"Mind the broken glass, now," says McCloy. "I'll send Mike to sweep it up."

"Be sure to put it on our bill," says Douglas. "The glasses."

They sit in embarrassed silence while the barman whisks the shards of glass into a dustpan. Douglas tosses back his Scotch to rid his mouth of the blood and wishes he had a glass of water.

"Who does this belong to?" asks the barman, picking the Sony Walkman up from the tiles and holding it out. Douglas nods to the absent chair at the table.

"Is it broken?" asks Clare in a timid voice.

"Afraid so."

When Joseph returns to the table, everything is in order again. The broken glass has been taken away, and his Walkman reposes at his place, next to the half-full bottle of Budweiser. Extra glasses have been removed, the ashtrays emptied and returned. Douglas waits uneasily to see if Joey will speak first, but Joseph merely puts his Walkman in the pocket of his sheepskin jacket and inquires, after a pause of seemingly interminable length, if anyone has called for the check. His voice is reasonable, even pleasant.

"I think it's time to go," he says.

22

The Upsetting Incident

With the check, the barman brought them each a steaming Irish coffee. "Compliments of the owner," he said, resting his tray on the table and placing a tall mug before each of the hacks. He left the check discreetly, face down, in the center of the table, and withdrew.

Clare knew, immediately, that the Irish coffees contained no Irish whiskey, and thought again of McCloy's fine instincts. In his remote and guarded way, he was continuing to take care of them, protect them, while allowing his writers to save face. His small act of charity cheered her as nothing else could do; even before she lifted the mug to her lips she felt a measure of sobriety return.

Sigrid, too, was pleased. Her practical hand had been snaking out to examine the check, but she stayed it and lifted her mug. "Cheers," she said. Douglas and Joseph were more tentative. Clare guessed that Douglas, who winced as he drank, was glad for this reprieve, but Joey—anxious to make a clean getaway—stared at his mug with hostility. Clare willed him to lift the Irish coffee to his lips and partake of the gift; it seemed terribly important that they all drink a wholesome cup together before disbanding.

"Please, Joey," she heard herself saying. "Please drink. It's good. It will make you feel better."

"I really don't want any, Clare. I've never liked Irish coffee."

"But it's not the real thing. It doesn't have any whiskey in it."

"It doesn't?" Douglas, speaking for the first time since the debacle, possessed the voice of a stranger. It was a tight and constrained voice, somehow a register higher than it had been. He cleared his throat and said, gruffly, that McCloy was a crafty bastard.

"Please, Joey," begged Clare. Some of the profound terror she had felt during the brief brawl was beginning to return. She knew, had always known, that violence in any form could cow her, turn her into a supplicant, but her fright at the ludicrous battle that had taken place in Eugene's back room was not for the aimless combatants and their possible injuries. No. Much as these horrified her, much as she felt tears springing from her eyes at the first thud of fist on flesh, her overriding emotion had been one of aching loss. Never again would things be the same. Never again would the hacks be able to convene for lunch in the back room of Eugene's. There would be no T. J. Sperling Award celebration, no feeling of unity, no sense of thumbing one's nose at a world that refused to reward artisans, no chance to air the sort of grievances appreciated only by fellow hacks, no opportunity to practice the delicate and mysterious and infinitely involuted charms through which life was mysteriously strained and reinvented on the printed page. "Oh, please, Joseph," she said again. This time her voice was low and throbbing. It emerged, unbidden, as the voice of one of her heroines. She might have been pleading for sexual favors rather than asking a fellow hack to sample his drink.

"God, Clare! Don't have a fit, okay? See? I'm drinking." Joseph lifted his mug in his left hand and brought it unsteadily to his lips. Clare beamed her encouragement. As sobriety returned to them, so might a calm, rational atmosphere in which they could laugh at the events so recently enacted. They might, as her mother used to say, go home and have a good sleep and discover that tomorrow was another day. Clare did not think it possible for total forgetfulness to occur—they weren't that drunk—but for the first time she began to see possibilities for an amicable truce.

"Clare is playing mommy," said Douglas. There was no rancor in his voice. He said it affectionately. Sigrid lit a cigarette, and by the flare of the match Clare spotted blood on Douglas' lip. If she, myopic as she was, could notice such things, she assumed the others were fully cognizant of his injury and discreetly chose not to mention it. Her concern for Joey now shifted in the direction of his opponent; it seemed unbearable to her that Douglas, like an old warrior, should smile and lift his cup to them, unaware of his battle scars. Ice ought to be applied to his lip, and probably to Joey's right hand, which he was not using. What if it was broken? How would he type? Clare had heard of fights in which men broke their hands throwing the kind of punch that seemed so effortless in movies and fiction.

If Hawk and Slatts had somehow wandered into each other's novels and engaged in a barroom brawl, they would emerge whole, if rumpled, and wake up on the morrow to pilot tanks, solve crimes; Joseph and Douglas would wake with bruised knuckles, cracked lips, throbbing temples, and a sour taste in their mouths. She couldn't possibly broach the subject of their injuries, though. Merely to mention the farcical fight would endanger the fragile peace they seemed to be enjoying now. She glanced at Sigrid, to see if she had noticed the blood on Douglas' lip, but Sigrid was looking remote. Instinctively, Clare knew what Sig would say. She would not find the sight sad; she would murmur to Clare that Douglas was, after all, a vampire. He had sucked Joey's blood, provoking him to attack, and now he wore the badge of his savagery unknowingly. That was what Sigrid would say.

"*Yew*-geen!" came a shriek from the bar. "It's hailing out there! Martin says there's hailstones big as chestnuts!"

Clare put her glasses on. A man—presumably Martin—had just entered the bar and was brushing at his raincoat in an aggrieved manner. Some of the patrons ran to the windows and peered out. Yes, came the general cry, it was true. Hailstones pelted from the skies and came clattering down on Broadway. They lay thick in the gutters and bounced from the canopies sheltering the new quiche cafés. "Like golf balls," someone said. McCloy smiled and spread his hands, as if to abdicate responsibility for the weather, Clare thought. A man for all seasons. In the sudden silence, they could hear the hailstones striking metallic surfaces with a pinging, musical sound.

"Beware the Ides of March," said Sigrid. "The old soothsayer was right. The one with the dyed red hair."

"Not to worry," said Joseph briskly. "There are no princes present."

When beggars die, there are no comets seen; The heavens themselves blaze forth the death of princes.

Clare remembered the lines from a college production of the play, in which she had played not Calpurnia, but Portia.

"No princes here," said Joseph.

Douglas, who had been sitting quietly in his shrunken, wounded state, made a sudden motion so dramatic that for one dreadful moment Clare thought he was having a heart attack. His hand leaped to his chest and then, apparently not finding what it wanted, began a furtive yet determined search in the capacious inner pockets of his Harris tweed jacket. He withdrew *Fiona's Folly* and laid it on the table. "Listen now," he muttered, his hands once more wrestling with the contents of the pocket, "listen. I have something to tell you."

Awkwardly, he extricated an object from its hiding place and held it to his chest. It was a book, bound in dark cloth.

"Goodness," said Sigrid playfully. "I thought you looked rather bulky today."

"Something upsetting happened to me earlier," said Douglas. "I wasn't going to say anything about it, but I've changed my mind." He continued to hold the book close, as if protecting its identity. "A trivial incident, really, but upsetting."

Clare's deepest impulse was to beg Douglas to shut up. Usually, she would suspect him of setting them all up for a joke, but she was perfectly sure no joke would be forthcoming this time. The lack of drama in his voice, his use of the word "upsetting" (a curiously female word for Douglas to choose), and the point at which he had decided to tell his story all convinced her of his serious intent. He had spoken in reply to Joseph's morose assertion: *no princes here.* It surprised Clare to see how very well she had come to understand Douglas in the years of alternate Tuesdays; operating from within some harsh and unnegotiable code of honor, Douglas was about to punish himself for the humiliation of Joseph. In the ordinary course of things, humiliating Joseph might seem fair enough to him, but he had provoked him to the point of taking such a quaint revenge, his humiliation was now doubled. An eye for an eye; an unveiling for an unveiling. It would do no good for Clare to try to stop him.

He was describing a branch library located, it seemed, a few blocks from Eugene's. He made them see it very well—the dilapidated shelves and sullen librarians, the unpleasant surprises to be found in the card catalog, the general air of decrepitude and aimlessness that pervaded the long, dim reading room. It seemed a place where upsetting things might well happen. Douglas' voice had a lulling effect, commanding them to listen, to shut out the din that had recommenced in the front room and ignore the ping of the glancing hailstones. Sigrid sat alertly, hands folded, like a child at her desk. Joseph was expressionless, but he was listening.

Having set the scene, Douglas explained how it was he had come to set foot in the branch library, for the first time, many months ago. He sauntered about the neighborhood to kill time. When he saw the library, he was reminded of some small point of research he needed to look up for one of his novels. He entered and made straight for the shelf of encyclopedias. The library, although depressed, was not so bad then as it had become, and when he had found out what he needed to know he strolled about, surveying all the books on the Best Seller shelf ("with a certain bitterness," he said, earning a laugh from Sigrid) and reading the notices on the community bulletin board.

"And then," he said, "I heard someone saying 'Excuse me' and a librarian came by, wheeling a trolley with books that had been returned. She began to put them back in place quite efficiently. I remember she had very long, tapering black fingers, and when she handled the books she was—not reverent, certainly—she was *competent*. They looked safe in her hands, and it was a pretty sight, somehow. I was engrossed in watching those hands as they tucked the books in so gently. I spent rather a long time just watching.

"Then it occurred to me she might think I was one of those library perverts, and, anyway, I didn't want to be late for lunch. Just as I was turning to go, she picked a book out of the trolley and held it up. I was a fair distance from her, but you know how it is with things you'd recognize anywhere. She was holding my book. This."

Douglas placed the book he had been holding to his chest in the center of the table. It was a medium-sized hardcover book, long since deprived of its dust jacket. Clare could not imagine what book it could be, or why Douglas called it his. Nobody touched it.

"I was so pleased to see it there," he continued. "So pleased to be in that library at the precise moment when somebody was actually handling it. I was even more pleased that it had come off the trolley, because that meant someone had been reading it.

"I knew it had been sold to the libraries, and at first I used to go around and look for it, but it always eluded me. I told myself that was a good sign. It meant the book was in a perpetual state of being *read.* Then one day someone told me—it was Frier, actually—that a lot of books never arrive at the branch libraries, or they get stolen. I never bothered to look any more. And here—in this seedy, out-of-the-way, depressed little neighborhood joint—here it was, alive and well and being *read*! Being handled with long, gentle fingers when it was at rest. It made me very happy."

Douglas paused in his narrative, and there was a long, uneasy silence. Sigrid cleared her throat. "May I?" she asked, nodding at the book. Douglas shrugged. Sigrid opened it to the title page without lifting it up and read, aloud, the words inscribed there: "*None of the Above,* a novel by Douglas Reville."

"It was my first," said Douglas.

"Was it about multiple choices?" asked Sigrid.

Douglas' bloodstained lip curled up with a hint of his old mocking style. "Sure," he said. "It was about the multiple choices facing a young man at the beginning of his life. The usual."

"You never told us you'd published a real novel," said Sigrid. "A hardcover."

"Listen, now," said Douglas. "Here comes the important part. "Every other Tuesday, when we meet, I have made it a point to go to that branch library before I come to Eugene's. It was a ritual, a pathetic one, granted, but it meant something to me. I went to visit my book, the way you'd go to see a kid you had to put in an institution. Sometimes it was gone, and then I was glad. Someone was reading it. Usually, though, it was there on the shelf. I never saw it on the trolley again. The librarian with the long fingers must have quit, or got fired, because she disappeared about a year after I'd first seen her."

"What made you check it out today?" Sigrid frowned, pressing Douglas for an answer.

"I didn't," said Douglas. "I stole it. I put it in my pocket and walked out." He lifted the book tenderly and offered it to Joseph. "Look," he said. "Just look at the poor son of a bitch."

Joseph shook his head, recoiling visibly. "Look, Clare," said Douglas. "Open it up."

Clare received the book and opened its pages with dread. The print was rather faded, but she could see no other evidence of ill-treatment. She thumbed through and noticed faint scribblings on page 132; farther along, an entire page had been ripped in half. Someone had wielded a magic marker to great effect on page 201, blotting out the text with a tag-name of the sort seen spray-painted in the subways. The graffito appeared with regularity after that point—CHUX 138 ST, in fact, obscured the concluding paragraph of the novel. A crude drawing of an ejaculating penis filled the space beneath the author's final words.

"Oh, Douglas," she said. "They've mutilated your novel. No wonder you're taking it home."

"If they hadn't done such a job on it, I could have patched it up and dropped it onto friendlier shelves. A better library, you know?"

"How disgusting," said Sigrid. "How sad." She and Clare were moved to stroke the book, as if to urge life back to its defaced and tortured pages. Clare thought their movements seemed part of a ritual; as women, they hoped to console Douglas by caressing the shell that had contained his words. Correction. Women of a certain kind. Only female soldiers of fortune would turn to the horse before the rider. Joseph stared at their busy fingers with a look of such bewilderment and sorrow that Clare despaired of ever making known her purpose through the medium of words.

We are comforting the book, she might have said, because we have no means of comforting the man.

23

Ponying Up

The hailstones stopped falling over Broadway, and the writers began to examine the check. It came to fifty dollars exactly, a suspicious sum. While it was infinitely greater than their usual tariff for an afternoon at Eugene's, it was not enough to cover four lunches and nearly six hours of drinking.

It fell to Sigrid, as usual, to sort out what each of them owed. Normally her job was easy—a simple division of Bloody Marys (still only two dollars at McCloy's) tacked on to cheeseburger or salad prices and democratically split four ways, with Joseph paying approximately a dollar less because he drank beer. Today Douglas had swilled costly Scotch and all of them had imbibed four times their normal amount. Sigrid's head swam as she tried to remember how many times her glass had been replenished; by her reckoning she had been responsible for a quarter of the check in Bloody Marys alone. It was difficult even to recall what everyone had eaten, because it seemed so long ago. Eugene's scrawls revealed nothing.

"Did you have a cheeseburger, Clare?" Sigrid asked wearily.

"I think so," said Clare. "We must owe simply hundreds."

"Some of those drinks were on the house," said Sigrid. "Eugene is being far too generous, even so."

"I wonder if he remembered to add the round I wrote down on

the napkin?" Douglas seemed genuinely concerned. "I had a double that time—I charged myself twice."

"I hate to bring it up," said Sigrid, "but how about the broken glasses?"

Joseph produced two tens and laid them on the table with an eloquent look. He was assuming full responsibility for the ruined glasses.

"That's far too much, Joey," Sigrid told him. "Those glasses are purchased wholesale." It had occurred to her that a final embarrassment might still lie in wait. It was quite possible that the writers, even allowing for Gene's generosity, would not be able to pony up for the afternoon's excesses. Only Joseph seemed unconcerned.

"Can't we just split it four ways?" Clare's voice was poignant. Sigrid knew that it depressed Clare deeply to consider figures. "The way we used to?"

"I owe the most," said Douglas, "by far. I seem to be a bit short, but I'm sure Gene would put it on my tab." He rose manfully, preparing to cross over into the boisterous area of the barroom, but the realization that he did not really have a tab at Eugene's must have daunted him, and Joseph seized control.

"Sit down," Joseph said. "Congressman Enslow is paying for this afternoon. You can all just throw in what you can, and the congressman will spring for the difference. He'll also pay the tip."

"That's not fair," said Clare, who had been peering closely at bills extracted from her wallet.

"Do you have a better idea?" Sigrid, accustomed to lunching at Eugene's for under ten dollars, saw that she would have no carfare home if she paid her fair share. "We'll pay you back, Joey."

"I don't want to be paid back."

Sigrid remembered something he'd said earlier. "I thought you said you'd spent all your film-strip money," she said. "You said you were broke again."

"I lied. I signed up to do another one. It's called 'Understanding Teenaged Suicide.'"

"Oh, do be careful, Joey," said Clare. "It's so easy to get depressed, writing about tragic things. I nearly got sick researching the Inquisition for *The Spaniard's Woman.* Much better to stick with Hawk."

"Fuck Hawk," said Joseph cheerfully. "He's never around when you need him." He pulled more bills from his pocket and piled them on the table.

Sigrid added her ten. "Ante up," she said. "Put in what you can." Clare produced two fives and a single, Douglas laboriously counted out fourteen dollars. Sigrid, after some deliberation, left sixty dollars on the table and returned the rest to Joseph. "I've left ten for Gene," she said. "That's it, then."

Nothing remained for them to do but finish their Irish coffees, put on their coats, and go, but nobody made the first move. It was now, technically, the dinner hour, but the thought of food, even if she had had enough money to dine out, was distinctly unpleasant. She was reluctant to go home, unusual for her, and viewed the evening stretching ahead with small enthusiasm.

She was in the habit of eating alone. Except for the times when she allowed a man to take her out to dinner (and they were becoming fewer and fewer, for Sigrid did not like to encourage intimacy) she prepared her meal in the kitchenette of the Chelsea apartment and ate it in a chair near her window. With her meal she always drank one glass of wine. It was an inexpensive Italian red, purchased by the jug from the liquor store on the corner. Each jug contained precisely ten glasses. "I always know when ten days have gone by," the liquor-store owner told her. "You're regular as clockwork, sweetheart." There were three glasses left in the jug now. Since the thought of another drink tonight sickened her, she would surprise the owner by appearing one day late next time.

After her evening meal, she generally wrote at her typewriter for five or six hours. What if her motor skills had been sufficiently impaired to make her strike the wrong keys while typing? It was possible she would not be able to work on her new novel at all. She felt a sort of dread about the bleak hours stretching before her. Just when it was time to go to sleep, the day's drinking would be beginning to exact its toll; she would have a dull ache between the eyes, feel fatigue without drowsiness, long for the night to be over so she could once more find herself mistress of her orderly life.

Clare had begun to replace objects in her handbag, as if preparing to go. She slipped her glasses into the pocket of her down coat and smoothed her hair. Sigrid suddenly wished that Clare would invite her home to while away the rest of the dead evening. They could open a can of soup, brew a pot of coffee—Sigrid felt sure Clare would use real coffee instead of instant—and watch something bad and silly on television. They might talk, not about writing or writers, and make each other laugh. It was just possible that they might arrive at a point where real confidences could be exchanged—Sigrid would tell Clare about Lily, for example, or about her master plan.

But no. Clare, of course, would be rushing home to her apartment because someone else expected her company tonight. Clare had a lover—what had she said his name was?—who was, by her own account, as troublesome and tiring as Laird Bruce. Chris. Christopher.

"Are you seeing Chris tonight?" Sigrid asked, reaching back for her jacket. Clare's face turned toward her slowly; in her eyes was a polite, bewildered refusal to acknowledge the words. It was as if Sigrid had spoken out of turn and offended her. Perhaps she'd been drunker than she seemed and had forgotten mentioning him, or perhaps she thought it was none of Sigrid's business. The long, protracted lunch was over, and so—Clare's expression seemed to say—was the possibility of friendship. Sigrid felt rebuked, and it was a sensation so rare for her she felt it much more keenly than anything else she had been asked to feel that afternoon. In confusion, she pulled her jacket from the back of the chair and busied herself with the movements of departure.

When she looked up again, Clare was shaking her head and smiling ruefully. She seemed almost ashamed. She brought one hand up to shield her face, then laughed so softly Sigrid wondered if it was, indeed, a laugh.

"I'm sorry, Sig," said Clare. "I didn't understand at first."

"It isn't any of my business. I don't know why I asked."

"But it *is* your business. Of course it is." Clare pulled distractedly at her hair, her shoulders shaking. Yes, she was laughing. The many drinks had done their work.

"The thing is," said Clare intensely, "I see him *every* night. He just won't go *away*. It's remarkable."

There were a thousand rejoinders to Clare's complaint, but Sigrid did not think it was her place to present them. Her place was waiting for her, and it was not the place's fault that Sigrid did not wish to return to it.

They were securely zipped and buttoned in their outerwear now. Ready to go. Douglas' book disappeared, with all its sad secrets, into the Harris tweed, and the table was wiped clean of their presence. The mugs and ashtrays might have belonged to anyone, been the debris left in the wake of any random party drinking at Eugene's. Even the Harp coaster bearing Joseph's design for the Writers' Liberation Army had been removed. No sign of the hacks' tenure remained here; nothing distinguished this table as a place where hacks had lunched.

Just as they had all scraped their chairs back, preparing to rise, the pay phone in the corridor leading to the lavatories rang. Sigrid could not remember ever having heard the phone ring before. She glanced toward the bar and saw that the official phone was in use.

The barman called Mike was holding the receiver out and beckoning to the man who had first told them all about the hailstones. The pay phone rang once, twice, and nobody heard.

"I'll get it," said Clare. Shapeless in her down coat, she walked steadily toward the shrilling phone. For the first time, Sigrid saw that Clare was wearing high-heeled boots. They all watched her lift the receiver from its hook. Politely, Clare inclined her head and listened. It was not possible to hear her response. She turned, leaving the phone dangling by the cord against the wall, and went rapidly into the front room. Sigrid watched her making her way through the knotted crowd at the bar, being jostled by good-natured patrons who turned to apologize, surprised at finding her in their midst. She could see Clare's mouth open, knew she was trying to call to Eugene.

"What now?" Douglas murmured.

"Maybe," said Joseph, "we are destined to remain here forever. It is possible that those who come to Eugene's on the Ides of March are never permitted to leave."

Douglas laughed and made an allusion to "The Twilight Zone." It was the first conversation they had had since Douglas' confession. Sigrid felt she could not turn and watch them groping their way toward a truce, but she listened.

"Meet four journeyman writers," said Douglas, "who are under the impression that they have come to a saloon on Manhattan's West Side for a companionable lunch—"

"To share experiences, air grievances, and buoy each other up," said Joseph.

"Little do they know—no, that's not right—how *can* they know that this particular lunch will last for all eternity? The check will arrive, but it can never be paid, because the writers have chosen to lunch . . . in The Twilight Zone."

Clare had succeeded in alerting McCloy. Together, they navigated the room in a zigzag course, forging toward the pay phone. Clare's face was anxious, pale. McCloy's, as always, was unreadable. Sigrid could hear Joseph and Douglas chuckling behind her back.

"*No Exit* was written," said Joseph, "as a direct result of Sartre's experiences with Parisian traffic cops."

McCloy brushed past them on his way to the phone. At close quarters Sigrid could see that his face was not so unreadable, after all. He looked grim. "What's happening?" Sigrid whispered to Clare, who was now by her side. "Has something happened?"

But Clare seemed not to have heard. Her expression, if anything, was grimmer than Eugene's.

24

A Matter of Life and Death

The woman's voice had been low and reasonable at first, if slightly slurred. She had sounded Irish, or rather, like someone who had once been Irish. Clare could make little sense of the call; all she knew for sure was that a real event was taking place, involving real people. A mortal woman may or may not have taken her life, or tried to take her life, and that woman may or may not be, or have been, Eugene's wife.

The life of the bar did not diminish or mute itself while its owner coped with the voice at the end of the pay phone. Beneath the paper shamrocks Gene's customers drank and shouted and laughed, pounded their fists on the bar for emphasis, darted out into the street to see if the hailstones had melted, and fed coins into the pulsating jukebox, which was even now belting out a disco tune hard on the heels of a sentimental rendition of "Danny Boy."

The hacks had withdrawn, with native delicacy, to a sort of no-man's zone between the bar and the back room. Clare huddled with them. They all felt the need to give Gene privacy, but at the same time they could not, now, leave.

"Would you kindly fetch Mr. McCloy?" the voice had asked Clare without preamble. "It's very important, miss. Tell him Nora is in a bad way. She's expected to live—I think she is—but she needs to hear from him. That's if she *can* hear, poor soul."

"Who is this?" It had been a plea; Clare might have been seeking the identity of an obscene phone caller. "Please—who is this?"

"It's a neighbor, miss. Calling under the auspices of Suicide Prevention." The voice had faltered with the word "auspices," but in the next sentence it gained authority and flowed sternly down the wire. "He's still legally married, you know. No amount of blandishments from fancy women like yourself can change that. If you think he's going to marry you, you've got rocks in your head, miss. Ask Margie Egan, who used to hang out at the old Connemara. Ask that Eyetie woman from Astoria!"

"You're making a mistake—"

"Just bloody go and get him, girl. It's a matter of life and death."

Clare, the messenger of doom, glanced furtively at McCloy now, but his back was to the writers and his position told her nothing. It seemed he had been talking for some time. If his wife had tried to commit suicide, seriously, wouldn't he be off the phone and in a taxi now, speeding to her side? Or perhaps Mrs. McCloy had expired during the course of the conversation. "Keep talking," Clare whispered to the others. "We don't want to seem to be eavesdropping."

"Poor Gene," said Sigrid. "In all the scenarios we dreamed up for him, we never gave him a crazy wife."

"Don't talk about *him,*" begged Clare. "It's indecent." There was a long silence. In the bar, a heavy woman in a quilted vest raised her voice in indignation. She informed her friends that there was to be no green stripe painted on Fifth Avenue for the St. Patrick's Day Parade this year. A loud chorus of boos went up. Joseph cleared his throat.

"I've been thinking," he said. "I'd really like to read your book, Douglas. *None of the Above.*"

"I would, too," said Sigrid. "Such a clever title. Was it well received? Were there reviews?"

"It was reviewed in the *Times* together with three other first novels," said Douglas. "I can quote the last paragraph, if you like."

"Fair is fair," said the angry woman's companion. "This city was built on the backs of the Irish."

"Hold on now, Mick," said a tiny woman who had been obscured by the larger people around her. "I don't think you've got all the information. I read where they're not going to paint the line because it's supposed to rain. They use the latex paint, you know, and it would melt away in the rain and make a mess."

"That's what *they* say. *I* say they're too cheap."

"Ask Gene, he knows all about it."

"He's on the phone."

"No, he's not. Where is he?"

"The pay phone back by the johns."

"What for?"

"It seems astounding," said Douglas, quoting from his review, "that a man so young could encapsulate, so movingly, the lessons it has taken many of us half a century to learn. The elegance of his prose is instinctive and sure, but it is his wisdom and compassion which lift *None of the Above* from the ranks of the first-rate to that small, exalted niche wherein we place works of true art. Reville bears watching. It is too early to say that he possesses genius, but he has given us a first novel which is very nearly great."

"God," said Joseph softly. "God, Douglas."

"If I had a hat, I'd take it off to you," said Sigrid.

"That's the best review I've ever heard," said Clare.

Douglas smiled. "It's not bad, but I've written better ones."

The man called Mick came toward the back room, heading for the lavatory with a purposeful stride. He clapped McCloy on the shoulder as he passed. Clare wondered if he could be half of Mick &

Mary, but it seemed unlikely. He was too old. Beside her, Douglas appeared to be shaking with laughter. "You *believed* me," he wheezed delightedly. "I can't believe you *believed* that shit. How's your hand, Joey?"

"Pretty bad. I think it may be broken, but I can't tell. There's an emergency room near my apartment. I'll just drop in before I go home." His voice was curiously cheerful. "What did the review really say?"

"Although there are patches of genuine wit in *None of the Above,* Mr. Reville suffers from a disease common among bright, young, first-time novelists—he is self-consciously clever. Worse, in scenes meant to be taken seriously, he delivers a good deal of unintentional humor, as in the lugubrious chapter chronicling the suffering of gifted people in an indifferent society. Never mind, though. There is much to appreciate in this first offering and it would be mean-spirited to suggest otherwise. Doubtless Mr. Reville will learn to temper his youthful prose excesses and give us something to consider seriously next time around. He bears watching."

Clare stroked Douglas' arm, surprised at how easy it was to feel love for him. It was a love that could never last more than a few minutes but, as the reviewer had said, never mind.

"What snotty bastard wrote it?" Joseph inquired loyally.

Douglas named a woman reviewer they all liked and respected. "She was absolutely right," he said.

McCloy replaced the phone and turned slowly. Clare's throat narrowed in fear and she squinted desperately in an effort to make out the expression on his face. "How does he look?" she whispered, but no one heard. He came toward them, swimming slowly into her line of vision. He halted three feet away and regarded the writers with a look of surprise.

"Still here?" he asked. "I thought you'd gone." His tone was gentle, even if the words might have sounded curt. Clare tried to remember what she had told him about the call. How could he imagine she would breeze out without waiting to see if his wife was alive or dead? But of course she had, in cowardly fashion, merely said a neighbor wanted urgently to speak to him. "About someone called Nora," she'd added, not wanting him to think she knew too much about his life.

"Is everything all right, Gene?" Douglas asked.

McCloy shrugged, as if embarrassed. "I'm sure it's fine," he said, averting his face from the table, which had not yet been cleared. Clare realized he thought Douglas had been referring to the amount of money left.

"What we meant," said Clare, "was everything all right at home?" The awkwardness of her phrasing betrayed her agitation. "We meant—about the phone call."

"*Yew*-gene!" called a voice from the bar. McCloy glanced toward his customers, made an appeasing gesture with his hands. "Yes," he said in a distracted tone to Clare, "oh, yes. Don't trouble yourself."

"If there's anything we can do—" Joseph's voice trailed off to a self-conscious halt. McCloy was so obviously anxious to return to the bar that the writers suffered a sense of rudeness and superfluity in detaining him. Clare felt it keenly, but she could not leave without some assurance, some small token that would allow her to abandon him in good faith. She thought it possible that Gene, in his goodness, did not wish to burden them with dreadful news. It was certainly his right to maintain his dignity, not to make them privy to some sordid scene of bungled self-murder, now under control and already destined to become another chapter in what she thought of as the tragic volume of his unhappily married life. It was his right to go unbadgered by the luckless woman who had happened to cross into that life, telephonically, for several hectic minutes, but it was *her* right to be granted some small confidence.

Skillfully, with small propelling movements of his capable hands,

Eugene was shepherding them out of the back room. He appeared to be strolling with them in a country garden. "I'll be seeing you in two weeks, then?" Always, he asked this question, but this was the first time he seemed to doubt the answer. Clare was touched. The awkward fight had made its mark on him; he, too, had been afraid that things could never be the same.

"Definitely," said Douglas. "Our next meeting is a very important one, Gene. The T. J. Sperling Award is presented two weeks from today."

They were in the maelstrom now, threading their way through masses of reveling drinkers. The diminutive woman who had spoken of latex paint regarded the passing parade with undisguised curiosity. Joseph and Douglas began to discuss alternate routes home. "But I don't have any choice," Joseph was saying. "There's only the IRT for me." Sigrid said she preferred to take a bus, even if it meant she would not arrive home for hours. Clare, who was planning to walk the twelve blocks home, felt she was traversing the Last Mile. The door loomed; she would be cast out of Eugene's forever if she did not say something. He seemed to be taking them all the way to the door, as if eager to dispatch them into the unfriendly night.

"Happy St. Patrick's Day, Gene," Joseph said. "Have a good one."

"Happy St. Patrick's Day," echoed the others.

"And to you," said McCloy. "Thank you for the copy of your book, Sigrid."

"It was nothing," said Sigrid. "Literally."

She could bear, thought Clare, to live her entire life without knowing the identity of Mick & Mary, Bernie & Angelo; she could even endure going to her grave without ever being enlightened on the matter of Margie Egan and the Eyetie from Astoria. What was insupportable to her was the thought of failing to show Gene a measure of her esteem and friendship on such a calamitous day. She hung back so she would be the last to pass through the outer door.

"Gene," she said in a low voice. "Please tell me. Will your wife be all right? Will she recover? We didn't mean any harm, Gene, honestly we didn't. It was just one of those things."

His amazed look seemed contrived. How clever he was! Even now he sought to spare her! The decent blue eyes—not electric and flashing, but a nice pedestrian blue, rather like the color of a policeman's shirt—blurred over with the need to conceal their emotion.

"You haven't done any harm," he said at length. "You're confused, Clare. No harm done."

"But I care!" Clare wailed. "Don't mistake me, Gene—I do care!"

"Go home, now, Clare. Go home now, dear. You've had too much to drink. I'll see you in two weeks. We'll have a fine time then, won't we? It will be the day of the Sperling Award."

Sigrid's firm hand caught the arm of her coat, and Clare was conveyed, with the others, into the street.

"Whew!" cried Joseph, executing a little puppetlike dance on the pavement. "It's fucking cold out here!"

25

The Verdict

"Will we be seeing Mrs. Noonan Thursday night?" tiny Rose Flanagan asked.

"Nora will be here," said McCloy. "It's the one night of the year she comes into the city."

"Such a handsome woman, I always think. She must have been a beauty as a girl."

"That she was, Rose."

"She's had a hard time of it, I understand. Life has not treated her kindly, but Mrs. Noonan is just as sweet and considerate as if—" She searched for the proper metaphor. "As if it *had,*" she said. "Your sister is an angel, Eugene. Mrs. Noonan is as fine a woman as I've ever met."

No—it's me, you bloody fool. I dialed this phone because they've been hanging up on me all day.

But we've sorted it out, now, Nora. Don't you remember? It was all a mistake.

Imagine telling me to call the Suicide Prevention. Don't they know I'm RC?

Nora was calling yet again, she'd explained, to apologize for her earlier behavior. She was much soberer now, she told him, having made herself a pot of tea. She couldn't imagine why that bloody slut had come over all anxious about the call. Possibly it was guilt. At any rate, she wanted him to know there was a letter from his niece, no-good Bernadette, which she had left on his bed. *If she's asking for money again* [said Nora] *to hell with her. If you send her one cent, you're a fool. She made her bloody bed when she moved in with that Eyetie—now let her lay in it.*

"Such abundant hair," Rose was saying. "And the color, I'm sure, is her own. Real Irish hair, Mrs. Noonan has."

"Excuse me, dear," said Eugene, and went to settle the Ryan's bill. If they were leaving, then it must be eight-thirty. McCloy had often reflected that if clocks had never been invented, he would still know the time by the actions of his customers. When the cloth caps came in, it would be ten o'clock. Midnight was heralded by Rose's assertion that it was time to go, one A.M. by her actual departure, one-twenty by the reentry of Mick Flynn, who always walked her to her door and then returned, and so on. His day had been thrown out of joint by the hacks' decision to remain for so long. McCloy had forgotten to eat, and now there would be no chance to do so until he went home. His hollow stomach seemed only a fraction of the general hollowness his body was registering—missing his supper (taken, on Tuesdays and Thursdays, at a coffee shop on Amsterdam while Mike tended bar in the dead hours) was a very small part of it. The odd behavior of his writers had created the larger emptiness, for he craved information that would never be given him. What had precipitated the fight between Douglas and Joseph? Why was Clare so emotional, apart from the unusual amount of drink she had consumed, in her parting moments? What had passed between his hacks and his sister to propel Nora to such a pitch? He would never know. The destruction of the wonderful little instrument belonging to Joseph pained him also. It was a dangerous machine, urging listerners to think of things best forgotten, but it had not deserved to die so untimely on the tiles of his floor.

"The stocking shop is going," said a man named Byrne who kept tabs on the fortunes of the block. "I heard their lease runs out in June."

"A tiny wedge-shaped store," said Rose. "What will they make of it, do you think?"

Not since the time he'd spent odd nights at Margie Egan's had Nora acted so badly. Her capacity for mischief had been so great, during those months of his affair with the widowed Mrs. Egan, that he had concealed from her utterly his later liason with Connie LoCicero of Astoria. Why now, when he was innocent of fleshly sins—a hardworking middle-aged man who only wished to make his establishment a success—did Nora monitor him so closely?

"What I want to know," said Mick Flynn in reasonable tones, "is how can a dead man be Grand Marshal of the Parade?"

"It's the spirit of the thing," said Mary Boylan. "It's honoring an Irish patriot."

"It doesn't look right, having a man who's dead being the Grand Marshal."

"You're missing the point, Mick."

"I'm not."

"You are. He's missing the point, isn't he, Gene?"

"Gene's busy, girl. Ask Michael. He'll tell you."

"No, he won't. Mike's too young, he's like all the young folks, no respect for tradition."

"The Grand Marshal was young," said Rose meaningfully. "He was in the flower of his youth."

"Fuck youth," said Mick. "It's an overrated condition."

"The days of my youth were radiant," said Rose. "Beyond measure."

Unbidden, a perfect woman was assembling herself for McCloy. As he pulled the tap, ignoring his grumbling stomach, she took shape, like a jinni rising from a bottle. He thought he recognized the long legs of Pat, the resilient breasts of Connie, as she flitted by him.

She was composed of many parts. Surely the sweetly indented marks on the buttocks belonged to Margie Egan, and the glorious hair (a flaming banner, as Clare and Sigrid would have it) was Nora's. Her eyes were myopic and pleading, the eyes of Clare Connolly as he had last seen them. Even Bernie, his niece, was present; she made herself known to him by means of her toes, those pale and orderly digits he had once admired within the showcase of her sandals. The composite specter was rising fast, too fast. He wanted to crane his neck back for a final look, but he could not allow himself to behave so irrationally in full view of his customers. He felt it hovering over the bar in benediction, and then he sensed that it had gone. He hoped he wasn't turning peculiar.

"Tell me," said Mick Flynn, his voice unnaturally loud in McCloy's ear. "Who were the characters? Them who left, from the back room?"

"Hooligans," said Mrs. Flanagan. "They had a bit of a dustup, if you noticed." She glanced excitedly around her. She, too, had wanted to know who the strange people were, but it was not her way to elicit information about those whom she had never met.

"Out-of-towners," guessed Mary Boylan.

"Whoever they were, it doesn't look nice, does it?" Rose turned to Mary. "In a cozy place like this, and Eugene keeps it so nice, to see grown men bashing away at each other, breaking glasses and using rude language? And their women! The dark one looked like a madwoman to me, with her great staring eyes. Were they part of a biker gang, do you think?"

"No," said Mick contemptuously. "Jesus, woman—they weren't no Hell's Angels. I talked to the older fella for a while."

"I noticed," said Rose.

"He was on about politics and football, but he didn't make much sense. Unstable fella."

"I read something in the paper said there are thousands of crazy people wandering the streets, pumped full of drugs. They haven't enough hospital beds to cope," said Mary Boylan. "You want to watch it, Gene. Customers like that could give the place a bad name."

That really was enough, thought McCloy. His poor hacks, subjected to a kangaroo court in their absence, had to be defended. "Don't upset yourself," he said. "I know them well. They come here every other Tuesday. It's a sort of club they have, a *tradition.* Today they stayed on, had a bit too much to drink, that's all."

Mick suggested they were from the ranks of the unemployed, frittering away their benefits on drink.

"They're writers," said McCloy.

"What do they write?" Mrs. Flanagan was instantly alert, jealous. Her nephew occasionally contributed pieces to the *Irish Echo.* Until this day she had considered herself the only conduit through which literary activities might be funneled into Eugene's.

"Books," said McCloy. "Novels and such. Mostly novels."

"I wouldn't have thought it," said Mary. "Not to look at them. Are they famous? Have we ever heard of them? I've never seen any of them on the TV."

McCloy thought of *Fiona's Folly,* safely secreted in its niche, and of all the other brightly bound, garish books handed over the bar to him, each suitably inscribed. His secret library. There was a time when folk who drank in places like his would show a token respect, evince modest awe at the evidence that anyone, anyone at all, could write words on paper and see them committed by some mysterious process to the printed page. The time was surely past. Nothing short of appearances on television talk shows would persuade his customers that the hacks were anything but drunken hooligans.

"No," he said. "They're not famous. You've never heard of them."

"Why do they bother, then?" asked Mary.

"A person has to eat."

"They could get honest work, couldn't they? They're young and able-bodied."

"It's what they know how to do," said McCloy. "It's what they do best."

"Imagine that!"

"If it's stories they need, I've got plenty," said Rose. "My life is a book. I've often thought if anyone could write the story of my life, they'd be rich."

"If my walls could talk . . ." Mary let the words trail off with exquisite humor.

"Seriously," said Mick Flynn, "if one of them characters is interested, I'd recommend talking to my brother Denis. He's been on the force for fifteen years now. You wouldn't believe the stories he could tell you—best-seller stuff. He's always looking for someone to write it up for him."

"I'll pass the word along," said McCloy. He moved down the bar to see how his other customers were doing. It was a point of pride with him to see to their quaint needs; it was not enough simply to serve them their drinks and offer an occasional one on the house. Unlike Mike the barman—one of the younger generation who cleverly eluded the conversational traps set for him in his horizontal patrol—McCloy believed in establishing checkpoints along the way. He was, he thought, a landlord of sorts, and it was only right that every soul who entered his premises and spent hard cash for comfort be made to feel welcome.

Stomach grumbling with hunger, temples taut with the unexpected emotions dragged from him today, he found it difficult to fulfill his obligations gracefully. As he paced the length of the bar to see to a young couple he knew only as John and Sheila, he wondered how long it would be before they deserted him in favor of a canopied café full of hanging plants and waiters on roller skates.

Young Sheila had bright gold hair, nearly up to the standards of one of Clare's heroines. He smiled and bantered, pulled the tap. Mixed with his various bodily discomforts was a sensation midway between joy and pain. It could not be described as throbbing, much less volcanic or tumultuous, and it did not consume every fiber of his being, but it persisted. It was a gentle longing, quite inappropriate, which he did not intend to investigate.

"Yes," he heard Mrs. Flanagan repeating, "my life has been a book."

"You and me both," said Mary Boylan.

"If someone would only write it."